If only he hadn't called her "little one."

Deborah took a step forward, placing herself unnecessarily close to James, her attitude challenging. "I don't feel threatened, James, but perhaps you do?" And with that she moved fractionally closer.

She got the response she wanted. With a feeling of triumph Deborah parted her lips against the pressure of his mouth. She was determined that he would acknowledge her fully as a desirable woman.

Then in the recesses of her mind she knew a vague feeling of alarm as her pulses leapt and accelerated. She wanted more than an acknowledgment from James, she wanted *him!*

Deborah pulled away, alarm turning to fear, and he let her go at once. "No," he said quietly, "I don't feel threatened. But are you *quite* sure that you don't?"

Books by Claudia Jameson

HARLEQUIN ROMANCE

HARLEQUIN PRESENTS

These books may be available at your local bookseller.

A Time to Grow

Claudia Jameson

Harlequin Books

TORONTO • NEW YORK • LONDON
AMSTERDAM • PARIS • SYDNEY • HAMBURG
STOCKHOLM • ATHENS • TOKYO • MILAN

Original hardcover edition published in 1984
by Mills & Boon Limited

ISBN 0-373-02691-9

Harlequin Romance first edition May 1985

CHAPTER ONE

'BOTHER!' Deborah fished in the drawer for another pair of stockings in the same shade as the ones she had just put on, one of which she had laddered. She wasn't normally so clumsy ... Perhaps the arrival of James Beaumont was affecting her more than she would admit?

No, it wasn't that, she realised on inspecting her fingernails. The nail on her index finger was chipped slightly, and that was how she had managed to ladder her nylon. She took an emery board from her dressing table and did a repair job before opening another pair of stockings. She had never felt comfortable in tights, finding them constricting and ugly, and another advantage of wearing stockings instead was that two pairs normally had the life of three or four pairs of tights, since she always bought several pairs in the same shade. Not that she needed to think about economy when buying such small items. Come to think of it, she didn't need to consider economy when buying bigger items, either. She didn't need to think about economy, full stop.

Still, the only way she really indulged was in buying clothes, yet her wardrobe was not extensive; it spoke of quality rather than quantity. What did she need stacks of clothes for? She rarely chose to go anywhere special, so most of her clothes were bought with work in mind.

At the sound of a car on the drive she went to the window, forced to acknowledge, now, that James' arrival was bothering her considerably. But of course it was! Why did he have to come back, and why did he have to come here? she asked herself, even though she knew the answers. He was coming back to England

5

because he had had enough of working abroad and he was coming here, to Vale House, because this was her grandfather's house, and it was her grandfather's company he wanted.

Half-dressed, shielded by the curtains, she stood to one side of the window as she looked out. Her bedroom was at the front of the house, which was not overlooked, but she didn't want to risk being seen.

It was her mother's car, and within ten minutes she would come upstairs and would be knocking on Deborah's door, telling her about her day.

For the moment, Deborah stayed where she was, soothing her soul with the beauty of the view before her. Just a few miles west of Sheffield, near the border of South Yorkshire and Derbyshire, her grandfather's house stood on the edge of the Peak District with its miles and miles of beautiful greenery, forests, hills and dales and lakes, and she loved it all. She loved the district and the house. She loved the peace, the quiet of the countryside she was feasting her eyes on. Most of all she loved Vale House itself, a house which represented to her security and stability—such valuable anchors in life! There was so much to hold on to here, so much to cherish.

But how drastically her attitude had changed over the years, about all of this! Ten years ago, when at fifteen years of age she had moved in to this house with her mother, she had *hated* the place! She had hated the boredom of peace and quiet, she had hated the old, rambling house. She had hated her new school, her lack of friends here, and she had bitterly resented her mother for bringing her here. Here, of all places!

It had been bad enough learning of her parents' divorce, bad enough being taken from her boarding school and all her friends in Devon without being forced to live in a different county—almost a different country, it had seemed to her at the time. As for living with Sir Henry Wilson, Professor Sir Henry Wilson, the grandfather she had always been in awe of, well, that had been too much ... to say nothing of James Beaumont's presence.

Her eyes moved slowly downwards, back to the sweeping driveway and her mother's parked car, then she moved away from the window and finished dressing, her mind still going over the past as she did so, back to the time when she had been brought to this house. She had been so young, frightened, bewildered by the changes thrust upon her, by the news of the divorce, and she had been mortified when her mother had said that the only way Deborah would see her father again would be over her dead body.

She had never had the chance to be close to her parents, having been sent to boarding school because her father's job kept them overseas, but their divorce had affected her deeply. There would be no *home* to go to in the holidays, no more holidays as a *family*.

Then came the changes, all the strangeness of a new school, a day school, the unfamiliar northern accents, her unapproachable grandfather and the unhappy face of a mother who grew more withdrawn and bitter with every passing day. There had been these things, and the prospect of the eternal absence of her father. *And* there had been James Beaumont to make life even more unpleasant for her—deliberately.

In those days, at the most difficult time of her life, James Beaumont had been living in Vale House, a dark and intense man who spoke to her only in order to criticise her. Most of the time he was silent, watching, unsmiling, his very presence making her uncomfortable and self-conscious, making her feel as though she had no right to be there—when it was actually the other way round.

Unsympathetic, intolerant, and newly-qualified as a doctor—a doctor, of all things!—at twenty-five he had possessed not an ounce of understanding; he had even bullied her physically as well as mentally.

'Now, any minute now, he was coming back to Vale House, and Deborah had no reason to expect to find him a changed man. But she had been a teenager when he had last seen her, and he would find her very different indeed. She didn't hate him, despite the humiliation he had caused her more than once, but she did resent him and she certainly resented his coming to stay at the house for an unknown length of time. What right had he, really, to come and stay here? What unwelcome changes would he create in the household? Vale House was a happy place these days, everyone in it got on with their own lives and harmony had reigned for several years. She didn't want disturbance in her life of *any* kind.

'Come in.' She had finished dressing by the time her mother knocked and was sitting at the dressing table, taking the pins out of her hair.

'Hello, darling. You're looking very smart, as usual, but isn't that a little too—businesslike? Surely you'll be changing for dinner?' Louise Wilson-Courtney planted a light kiss on her daughter's cheek and she didn't wait for an answer, so Deborah didn't bother to tell her that she had in fact just bathed and changed her clothes. 'No sign of James yet?'

'Not yet. It seems he phoned Gramps this morning and said we should expect him between five and six. He flew in to London airport last night and a friend of his is driving him to Yorkshire.'

'That's nice.' Her mother sat gracefully in the lady's chair by the window. 'I'd have hated not to be here when he arrives. I'm so looking forward to seeing him, and my father's almost excited, I'm sure of it!'

Deborah was certain of it. She sighed inwardly. It seemed that everyone was looking forward to seeing James Beaumont, everyone from the family to the housekeeper, from neighbours and friends to the daily lady who hadn't even met the man! Her grandfather was responsible for this—this sense of anticipation in everyone. He had known the younger man for many years, and he adored him.

James had left England when Deborah was almost sixteen, when she had lived at Vale House for nearly a year, and she had been relieved and delighted to see the back of him. He went to America to work and to study further in a postgraduate teaching hospital in San Francisco. He had been back to visit only twice during the intervening years, once when she was eighteen and once when she was twenty-one—but she had not been around during his second visit.

Every month, religiously, during all the years since James had left Yorkshire, he and Sir Henry had exchanged letters. After completing his studies in America, James had been working with the World Health Organisation and his correspondence had come from several different countries. Sometimes his letters were late, through no fault of his own, no doubt, and Gramps would bemoan the fact and curse the backward postal systems in backward countries. But the letters always got to Vale House eventually, and Gramps would go off to the library to read them and reply to them.

Occasionally, when there had been an outstanding item of news about James, Deborah got to hear about it whether she wanted to or not—like the time when James had been shot in the leg, a few months ago, during a local uprising in some small African state. She had been obliged, then, to listen to her grandfather explaining the circumstances of what had happened, but for the main part she had shown no interest in the contents of James' letters.

Her grandfather had been knighted for his services and innovative contribution to the practice of medicine.

For many years a consultant orthopaedic surgeon, he had worked in Yorkshire hospitals and lectured to the students of Sheffield University Medical School—of whom James had been one. Now seventy-four years old, he had long since retired and it had been four years since he had seen the young man he was so fond of.

'What's Gramps doing?' Deborah asked of her mother, picturing him standing downstairs by the window, watching eagerly for a car coming up the drive. When you reach the age of seventy-four, she supposed, a four year absence must seem like a very long time. But she remembered only too vividly *her* last encounter with James—and in her case it had been seven years ago.

'He was feeding his fish when I came in.' There was just a tinge of impatience in her mother's voice, which annoyed Deborah no end, though she didn't show it. Since her mother's recent romantic involvement with a visiting foreigner, she had become less and less interested in the house and its occupants and more and more concerned with the man she was obviously hoping to get a proposal from.

'His fish are one of his pleasures in life,' Deborah pointed out.

'And cricket and his cronies, and soon it will be his rose garden—when summer finally arrives.'

'Soon it will be James,' Deborah amended.

Louise glanced at her via the dressing table mirror. 'Will you be jealous? Of James stealing your grandfather's time during the evenings?'

'Don't be silly, Mummy.' Yes, was the answer to that . . . if that's what James would do. But surely he wouldn't be sitting around the house all day and all evening? Surely he would be getting himself organised now he was back—finding a new position and a place to live?

'It'll be nice having a man around the house,' her mother went on.

Deborah paused as she gathered her hair together on the crown of her head. 'I don't think Gramps would be very flattered to hear that remark.'

Louise laughed. 'I meant it will be nice for *you*, darling. I mean, I certainly appreciate Hans being around so often, and I meant that it will be nice for you, having a young man around the place.'

'Young? James is ten years older than I am.'

'And you're twenty-five. Therefore James is a young man.'

'If you say so.' As far as Deborah was concerned, this conversation was becoming irritating, and it grew more so.

'You know very well in what context I was using the word "man",' her mother went on. 'Henry doesn't count. He's your grandfather and he's old. We can't think of him as a man in the context I was using.'

This provoked Deborah actually to turn around and stare at her mother. 'Well, I certainly can't think of James Beaumont in *that* context of the word "man", either!'

'How can you say that? It's four years since you've seen him and he always was attractive. I'll bet he's more so now, now that he's more mature.'

Attractive? Attractive! That dour, unsmiling person who had made her life a misery by telling tales on her? How could she be open to the suggestion of his being *attractive*? But she made no comment about her mother's opinion, she just started again with her hair, gathering it into an elastic band before arranging it into a tightly coiled knot.

'Why are you frowning like that, Deborah? What are you thinking?'

'That it's seven years since James and I met, not four.'

'Oh, yes! Of course it is. You weren't here when he last came to visit, were you? You were away on that antiques course.'

'It was called a Fine Arts course, Mother.'

'Was it? Mm. Well, you're the one with the excellent memory, darling. Anyhow, that means you were eighteen when James last saw you. How different he'll find you! You've changed so *much* since then!'

It was the first thing that Louise had said which actually pleased Deborah. Indeed she was a very, very different girl from the eighteen-year-old she had been when James last came to stay. Seven years had changed her a great deal; she only hoped she would be able to say the same thing for *him*.

Her mother was looking at her watch. 'Heavens, it's ten to five now! I must go and change, I don't want James to see me looking like this!'

Irritation again. Why shouldn't James see Louise wearing trousers and her painting smock? So what if he did? Good grief, it was like awaiting the arrival of royalty! He was causing a disturbance in the household before he had even got here!

Deborah checked that thought, knowing it was a gross exaggeration. There wasn't, nor would there be, any disturbance. Not to her, at any rate. Life would go on as calmly and as peacefully as ever—just the way she liked it. James Beaumont would be incapable of upsetting her these days. Incapable.

Her red-auburn hair, shoulder length and quite curly when loose, was now pulled back and securely tied into a coil on the crown of her head and she turned her attention to her make-up. Five minutes saw the completion of this task since she didn't wear skin make-up, just lipstick and a touch of shadow and mascara around her tawny-hazel eyes. She looked at herself critically, nodded, then moved to the full length mirror in her wardrobe in order to examine her reflection from head to foot.

This was something she did with a little more interest than she usually took, but in *her* case it was very important that she looked just right when she and James came face to face. It was important that he realised instantly that he was meeting a mature, level-headed woman, a woman who was very far removed from the naïve and idiotic teenager he had accused her of being on his visit seven years ago.

She was, now, a business woman who had made something of her life. She was self assured, no longer lacking confidence, no longer prone to outbursts of a temper he had once called 'uncontrollable'. On the contrary, her volatility had long since been harnessed and she was thought of, referred to, as being cool, calm and collected.

By her attitude and appearance she would set a precedent with James this evening and make an unspoken demand for the respect with which he must treat her if she were to tolerate him at all.

Her emerald green suit was just right. It was beautifully tailored and it fitted to perfection. The plain, navy-blue blouse made the perfect foil for it and matched the shade of her shoes. Her hair was immaculate, as was her grooming in general. She checked her nails again, making certain she had done a good job on them. Right! Now, she told herself, practise the friendly smile your grandfather will expect you to give his darling James, but don't let your eyes smile; friendly detachment is the expression you're after. That's it. That's perfect.

She went downstairs.

Gramps was in the drawing room, standing by the window and watching for a car on the drive, just as she had known he would be. For just a few seconds Deborah was actually glad that James was coming, because it was making her beloved grandfather so happy. As she looked at him, a little stooped now as he stood, her heart filled painfully with the enormous love she had for the man who had over the years become the very rock of her life, the best thing in her life. He had changed, too. He had once been awesome and unapproachable . . . and now he was her best friend.

The pain which came with the rush of love for him was based on fear and the fact that he was seventy-four, the fact that two years earlier he had suffered a mild stroke which had left him with only partial use of his left hand and arm. He was not getting any younger. She could think no farther than that, and that was enough to frighten her. He was not getting any younger. 'Gramps?'

He turned, smiling, his right arm extended as she walked towards him. 'Hello, love. I didn't hear you come in.'

Despite the stoop of his shoulders he was still far taller than she, by several inches. And in spite of his age and his handicap he was still as strong as an ox. She comforted herself with such thoughts often. She hugged him, leaning against him as his arm came around her shoulder and he turned back to the window.

'I came in an hour ago,' she said. 'You were snoozing in your armchair so I didn't wake you.'

Wise blue eyes looked down at her. With a shock of white hair, equally white and bushy brows and a walrus moustache, Sir Henry was vaguely reminiscent of Albert Einstein in his later years. Physically, that was.

Sir Henry came from an ordinary background in an ordinary family. He had never lost his Yorkshire accent, nor attempted to do so, and he was blunt and forthright, if not to say shocking at times. Deborah's friends and acquaintances thought him a little eccentric, but she didn't think so.

'I thought you'd have come home earlier today, knowing that James is coming.'

She smiled at him. 'I went to an auction, remember? I had——'

'Of course I remember,' he chided. 'But you didn't

have to go to the shop when you came back, did you? You could have put your new purchases on display tomorrow, couldn't you, and come straight home after the auction?'

'I did come straight home after the auction. The pieces I bought are in a box in my sitting room. I haven't been to the shop. And how do you know,' she went on, her smile widening, 'that I didn't leave the auction empty-handed?'

The wise blue eyes were laughing at her now, very crinkled at the corners. 'Because you're a determined little devil and you've already got a buyer for those antique pill boxes you wanted. How much did you spend?'

'Altogether? Fourteen hundred pounds.'

Sir Henry grunted, cuddling her against the warmth of his big body, and Deborah put her head on his shoulder, enjoying the familiar scent of him. She wished she could have had this sort of relationship with her grandmother, too, but Sir Henry's wife had died shortly before Deborah and her mother moved in with him. Her memories of her grandmother were few and far between, just isolated pictures of visits to this house when she was a child.

It was thanks to her grandmother, and her own antique business, that Deborah was financially independent. She had inherited a generous amount of money from her grandmother, which had been left in trust for her until she was twenty-five. Her grandmother had been a refined and beautifully spoken lady, a gentle person from a wealthy family. It was thanks to her wealth that she and Gramps had been able to buy this house some fifty years ago, when Professor Sir Henry Wilson was just plain Henry and a medical student with no funds of his own. The couple had been absolutely devoted to each other, according to Louise, and Sir Henry missed his wife very much indeed.

'Can I get you a drink, Gramps?'

'No. I'll wait till James gets here.' Her grandfather moved to the armchair, his armchair, which nobody else would dare to use, chuckling as he sat. 'Ten years, Debbie. I wonder whether he realises it's ten years this month since he left England? Almost to the day, as a matter of fact.'

'I'm sure he does.'

'It'll be so good to have him home, won't it?'

'I . . . wonder how long he'll stay with us?' She dodged the question, unable to bring herself to lie, unable to answer him in the negative.

'What do you mean?' Sir Henry used the tone of voice which once used to frighten her. It had taken her a long time to get used to the deep and booming voice which was at his command when he wished to use it. 'He's coming home for *good*. I told you what was in his last but one letter to me.'

'That he wasn't taking on any new appointments overseas. Yes, I remember,' she said softly. 'And I know he's going to settle and work in Yorkshire but—well, I just wondered how long he'd stay here in the house. Only, I hear that old Mr Wagstaff has put his cottage up for sale because he's going to move in with his son, and I thought James might like to know about that . . .' Her voice trailed off.

'What for? He'll be living here.' Sir Henry was pointing his finger downwards. 'This is his home. Why the devil should he look for somewhere else to live?'

It isn't his home, she wanted to say. He is not part of the family. He's a friend of the family, that's all, a friend you took under your wing many years ago. He's your protégé, but he does not *belong* here. 'Don't get excited, Gramps. It's just that I don't envisage James wanting to stay here for ever—after all, he's thirty-five and he's a bachelor . . .'

Deborah didn't need to say any more. She could

leave the rest to her grandfather's common sense, of which he had an abundance.

'So? You're twenty-five and you're a spinster, but you live here. Does the family get in your way when it comes to your love life? Nobody invades your privacy, and it will be the same for James. So why should he want his own place?'

'Darling, you can't really compare me with him——'

'How right you are!' he conceded gruffly. 'Because you don't even have a love life, come to think of it! Not only are you dead set against marriage, you don't even have a love life! You'll be living in this house when you're a very old maid!'

'Gramps! Honestly! I was only trying to spare you disappointment by pointing out that you shouldn't take things—James—for granted. He might not want——'

'At my age, you don't take anything for granted. James lived with me and your grandmother from the time he was seventeen years old—and I've known him since he was a small boy. Remember that. I know him far better than you do.'

Deborah wasn't so sure about that. Oh, he had lived with James for longer than she had, but she had seen sides of James' nature which her grandfather didn't know existed. Still, she let the subject drop. She was annoyed with herself; she had upset Gramps by talking about James leaving Vale House before he had even got here, and that was stupid and very tactless of her. 'You're probably right,' she said, smiling. 'After all, he couldn't possibly find a nicer place to live. And he's got you here.'

The old man looked at her with a mixture of amusement and suspicion. 'Don't patronise me, lass. Why don't you come right out with it and say you don't want him here?' He shook his head. 'Don't bother. But you were a child of fifteen when you first met James, and you were still a child when you last saw him, so I——'

'I was eighteen, a young woman of eighteen.'

'A child, still a child. And don't interrupt. I was about to tell you, to assure you,' he amended, his voice much gentler now, 'that your attitude will change when you get to know the man properly. You'll be meeting on an equal basis now—as two adults. You'll find him very different.'

'I doubt it.' She thought she had only thought the words, but she had voiced them.

Her grandfather was smiling now but there was a trace of worry in his eyes. 'You have a long memory, Debbie, just as I have. I can remember very clearly the animosity you felt for James. He didn't care for you, either, not that you need to be told! Yet he was kindness itself to you, if you'll just stop to think about it.'

She clamped her lips together. She was far from speechless but she was damned if she was going to lose her composure and dignity by entering into a row.

'She's flabbergasted!' Sir Henry made the statement with a bark of laughter. 'Now, I want you to do something for me . . .'

Deborah was sent on an errand to the cellar. The housekeeper, Bessie, was busy in the kitchen preparing a special dinner, and was not to be disturbed. So it was Deborah who had to go and fetch the red wine from the cellar—several bottles of Sir Henry's very best vintage. She had been told also to fetch two bottles of champagne and a bottle of the rare old Scotch he kept for extra-special occasions.

She put the champagne in the coldest part of the fridge and the Scotch on the kitchen table for the moment, and she was back in the cellar getting the wine when she heard the commotion in the hall.

The cellar door, beneath the main staircase in the hall, was open, and Deborah was half-way up the steps when she heard several voices talking at once, her

grandfather's being the loudest. She heard James' voice,
her mother's and that of another man, which she didn't
recognise.

The latter, presumably the man who had brought
James from London, was insisting that he couldn't stay
for a drink, that he had to press on because he was
expected in Leeds shortly.

Deborah put down the wine and waited on the cellar
steps, listening to the thanks, the cheerios, the welcome
homes being bandied about. She heard the excitement
in her mother's voice, the emotion in her grandfather's—
and then Bessie's voice joined the rest, briefly. She
heard James saying that what he wanted most of all was
a cup of tea, then she heard Bessie's footsteps passing
the cellar door as she hastily made her way back to the
kitchen. No doubt James would be served his tea within
five minutes.

'Four, if Bessie can manage it,' Deborah muttered to
herself, clicked her tongue and picked up the wine. As
the party in the hall moved into the drawing room, she
emerged and put the bottles on a nearby table, took a
quick glance in the hall mirror to make certain her
appearance had in no way been disturbed, then headed
for the drawing room.

There was no point in delaying the meeting for five
more minutes. Besides, Gramps would be disappointed
with her if she didn't put in her appearance quickly.

Seeing James was a shock to her. Physically, he had
certainly changed. He was even taller than she
remembered, and leaner, and his skin was so tanned it
was the colour of mahogany. Deborah's eyes were
compelled instantly to the face she had never thought of
as being attractive. But it was attractive. Now, at any
rate. In fact it was strikingly attractive, though
considerably leaner than it used to be.

He was standing by the fireplace, and in those split
seconds as he turned to face her fully, Deborah thought

that she could easily have walked past this man in the street and never recognised him.

James Beaumont!

As her eyes moved to his eyes, she knew instantly that the changes in him were more than physical. Of the darkest shade of brown, his eyes were filled with warmth and humour—things she had never seen in them before. Naturally he looked older but there was something . . . something about him that told her he had aged far more than seven years during the seven years since she had seen him. It was an impression which at this point she could not be more specific in defining.

He also looked genuinely pleased to see her. He was different—just *different*, and she had never seen him looking so dishevelled, almost to the point of scruffiness. He was dressed in an old, black leather jacket, a black roll neck sweater and faded denims. On his feet were a pair of leather sandals which had seen far better days, and he was badly in need of a shave. The shadow of his whiskers was as intensely black as his hair, hair which was thicker than she remembered. Gone was the side parting he once used to wear; it was brushed straight back from his hairline now, untamed and longer than she had ever seen it.

All this was what Deborah saw as she walked towards him, her hand extended. She was experiencing surprise, even a touch of suspicion, and when his face broke into a smile both these feelings increased dramatically. Against the deep bronze of his skin, his teeth were beautifully white and even. He was laughing now, and her gaze flickered to the intensely dark eyes which always used to look at her accusingly.

'Debbie!' James ignored the hand she had extended, his arms going around her in a demonstrativeness which at once startled and annoyed her. 'Well, well, well! Look at little Debbie!'

She stiffened, pulling away from his hug as rapidly as good manners would allow. But during the mere seconds in which he embraced her she was made aware of the solid, sinewy strength about him.

The smile of friendly detachment she had practised was now successfully put on display, even while she was irked by his gesture and irritated by his words. Little, she might be, compared to his height of six feet or more, but she found his patronising attitude unwelcome to say the least.

'Deborah,' she said lightly, straightening the jacket of her suit as she moved away from him. 'Everyone calls me by my full name these days. I much prefer it.'

'I see,' he said quietly, his eyes full of amusement.

'Sit down, lad, sit down!' Sir Henry waved towards a chair. 'You must be quite tired after such a long haul.'

Deborah sat by her mother on the settee. Only a minute had passed since she had walked into the room and set eyes on him, yet already she was disconcerted. James was suddenly an unknown quantity, a stranger who was not a stranger. She looked at him, picturing clearly the way he used to be, the way he used to look.

He was still standing, saying something about his journey from Africa the previous day, and Deborah was thinking it odd that now, at thirty-five, his general appearance was what one might have expected when he had been a student. But his appearance had been immaculate in those days, when in her kindest moments she had thought of him as being sickeningly goody-goody, with his quietly spoken voice and his enormous respect for Sir Henry—or 'the Professor', as he used to refer to her grandfather.

Deborah was back in the past now, her mind zooming back to a time when she was fifteen years old and James had humiliated her horribly in front of her new-found friends . . .

CHAPTER TWO

CHRISTINE WARWICK was the only girl with whom Deborah had got on well at her new school in the north. It was close enough to her new home for her to be able to attend as a day student, though there were times without number when she had had no wish to go back to Vale House in the evenings. Vale House was boring, as were the people in it. Sir Henry's wife had died a few months earlier and there was an atmosphere in the house so leaden with unhappiness that one could almost taste it. Louise Wilson-Courtney was newly divorced from Mr Courtney, Deborah's estranged father, and the lodger in the house was a medical student who was just completing his pre-registration, or internship, as other countries call it.

When the student was at home he was either sleeping or studying in his room. There was no one for Deborah to talk to. Meal times were silent affairs as far as she was concerned, though there were occasions when the dark-haired man would try to make conversation with her. But he always asked stupid questions and made stupid suggestions.

The house was big and filled with old furniture and ancient paintings, and its contents did not then include a television set. Nor was there a record player. There was a radio—which Deborah was always being ordered to turn down, either by her mother or by her grandfather. And James Beaumont got more and more bossy as the weeks passed, especially when he was taking a 'holiday' after finishing his training. He was at home all the time then, talking about going abroad to work and make further studies.

22

Deborah couldn't wait to see the back of him. He was always picking on her, as was her mother, and when she first brought Christine Warwick home for tea, both adults told her later, separately, that Christine was not the sort of friend she should have.

But Christine was fun. In an expensive private school full of young ladies (the sort of school Louise had always sent her daughter to), Chris was the only girl who had a bit of *life* about her. With her antics in the classroom and her secret smoking behind the bicycle sheds during lunch-time, she brought laughter and a sense of excitement and daring into Deborah's life.

Chris always had plenty of money to spend. Her father was a book-maker and gave her a generous allowance. Her mother was young and pretty and dressed in the latest fashions, and she didn't mind how much noise the girls made when they were in Chris's house.

So Deborah had spent more and more time at Christine's home, and Christine's older brother really liked her. He was the lead guitarist in a pop group which played in clubs and pubs in Sheffield and the surrounding towns, and he let the girls sit in on the group's rehearsals.

Deborah refused to give up her friendship with Chris, but in order to have any fun at all she was obliged virtually to lead a double life. She would tell her mother she was going to Christine's to do her homework—which was the only way she managed to get out of Vale House so much in the evenings.

So, after several miserable months, life had improved enormously for Deborah, thanks to Chris and Dave Warwick. Dave was nineteen, up-to-the-minute as far as fashions and music were concerned, but it wasn't Deborah's enormous crush on him which eventually spoiled things, it was James Beaumont's interference.

At fifteen, Chris and Deborah were too young to get

into pubs and clubs in order to see the pop group performing, but it was almost as good to be sitting in on the rehearsals. On this particular night, a Monday, the two girls got into Dave's van and went with him to a rehearsal at the drummer's house—at least, that's where the girls thought they were going. But they found themselves being taken instead to the home of someone else—a friend of Dave's who had the house to himself for the week while his parents were away on holiday.

'You're going to a party,' Dave announced, slipping an arm around Deborah's shoulder as he drove the van in the direction of Derbyshire.

Chris shrieked with surprise and pleasure while Debbie revelled in the possessiveness of Dave's arm around her. But she was as worried as she was excited. 'I'll have to be home by ten-thirty. Dave, will you make sure we leave in good time for me to get back?'

'Don't be so wet,' Chris admonished. 'So what if you're a bit late for once? What can they do? They're not going to throw you out, are they?'

'No, but——'

'Don't worry, Deb. I'll take you back in time,' Dave promised.

Deborah had honestly thought he would. Whether he had intended to or not, she didn't know to this day. But the evening had been full of surprises and it was only eight o'clock when they got to the party. The house was big, detached, and the walls were almost vibrating with the blast of pop music at a tremendous volume. Lights were flashing, the atmosphere was thick with smoke and people were milling around in every room— shouting to make themselves heard, dancing, laughing, drinking and having the time of their young lives.

The last thing Debbie wanted was to appear childish in front of Dave or a spoil-sport in front of her best friend, so she took the drink Dave fetched for her—and the next one, and the cigarette Chris offered her.

Time simply flashed by and it was with a great deal of reluctance, and a certain amount of muzziness, that Debbie realised she would have to leave the party in order to get home in time for curfew. She was dancing with Dave for the first time ever, and loving it, when she told him she would have to leave.

'Soon, love, soon.' He pulled her close just as the music changed to a slow smooch, and it was more than she could do to insist on leaving just at that point.

She remembered clearly the blond, greasy-haired boy who came up to them while they were dancing, handing Dave a thin, half-smoked cigarette. She remembered Dave insisting she try it, which she did because he wanted her to. She remembered copying the way he showed her how to draw the smoke into her lungs . . . but she did not remember where the time went to after that.

Suddenly she was relaxed, no longer wanting to go home because she was not concerned with the lateness of the hour. Here, there was fun, music, laughter, a sense of freedom she had never before experienced— and there was Dave Warwick's arms around her, his lips against her neck as they continued dancing . . .

And then there was James Beaumont.

Suddenly *he* was there, towering over her, shouting to make himself heard, his dark features lit with a fury Debbie could not understand. She defied him in the most reasonable way, telling him she would come home when she was ready to, and not before.

'Like hell!' he bellowed, 'You're coming with me. *Now!*' He grabbed hold of her wrist in a vice-like grip, yanking her away from Dave, who immediately intercepted.

'Hey, cool it!' He poked at James' chest, then tried to pull Debbie back into his arms. 'Take your paws off her. She's with *me*.'

James turned to Deborah. 'Go and wait outside. Get in the car, it's right outside the door.'

'No, I won't! I'm staying with Dave, and you can mind your own business!' James had ruined everything. People were looking, laughing.

'Yeah, why don't you mind your own business?' Dave moved aggressively towards James, who was far taller, far broader and far angrier than Dave was.

Dave didn't stand a chance. James didn't need to hit him; he just put the flat of his hand on the boy's chest and pushed, sending Dave sprawling to the floor.

Debbie was outside in a flash, but not before she shouted a stream of abuse at James. A circle of people had formed around them, the music was turned off and several jibes were flung in her direction, humiliating her beyond words.

'Overstayed your bedtime, kid?'

'Who's this? Your big brother?'

'Belt up, Pete, it's her father, obviously.'

She was still yelling at James when he scooped her high into the air and flung her over his shoulder in a fireman's lift. That was how she was carried out of the house, her arms beating against his back as the crowd's laughter rang in her ears. The instant he set her on her feet by the car, she kicked out at him viciously, her booted foot landing hard against his shin.

'Why, you stupid little bitch! Get in there!' He flung the passenger door open and shoved her inside, driving away with a screech of tyres and an acceleration that made her head spin.

'I'm going to be sick!' They'd driven barely a quarter of a mile and Debbie was sobbing with rage and frustration when she made this announcement.

James stood on the brake and leaned across her to push the door open. 'Then get out! You're not going to be sick in your grandfather's car.'

Ten minutes later she was back in her seat, sullen and white-faced. Her anger towards James was greater than anything she had known in her life but she was too shaky, too weak to give vent to it at that instant.

James was not similarly afflicted. He laid into her furiously with the lecture of her life. 'It's taken me two hours to find you, you little moron. Even Christine's mother didn't know where you'd gone. I've been from pub to pub to umpteen houses looking for you. What the hell do you think you're doing? And what's all that muck on your face? Where did you get those ridiculous clothes? You weren't dressed like that when you went out tonight. God help me, you're as high as a kite! How long have you been smoking grass?'

She looked at him stupidly.

'Answer me!'

'I—don't know what you mean. I don't——'

He shook her, hard. His eyes bored into her as he accused her of lying and he shook her until her teeth rattled. 'Don't lie to me, Debbie. The house stank of it. I'm well aware that you don't go to Christine's just to do your homework. I've seen you strolling round the town with a gang, made-up, dressed up in your funny clothes, but I had no idea you were this stupid! Who gives it to you? That boy you were with? And how long have you been mixing with the likes of him? Who is he?'

Deborah was frightened, shocked. She was thinking about the half-smoked cigarette. 'I swear—*honestly* I didn't know it was ... I've never smoked the stuff before. Honestly! I—oh, please, please don't tell anyone. You're not going to tell the police, are you?'

James just stared at her, his dark eyes glinting in the light of a nearby lamp. But when next he spoke, his voice was as quiet as it normally was. 'The boy, Debbie. Who is he, and how long have you been seeing him?'

'It's—he's Christine's brother. He's got a pop group and——'

'And you're one of his adoring fans!' He shook his

head, leaning one arm against the steering wheel. 'Has anything happened between you?'

Debbie lifted her head defiantly, misunderstanding completely. 'I love him.'

James laughed humourlessly. 'You don't love him. But that isn't what I meant. I want to know how much time you've spent alone with him and whether he's touched——'

'Shut up! No!' She snapped at him furiously. 'Dave isn't like that!'

'All men are like that.' He was searching her eyes and she met his gaze fully.

'You've got a dirty mind, James Beaumont.'

'And you're as innocent as the day you were born— thank God. Now you listen to me——'

She thrashed out at him and her arm was stopped in mid-air as she tried to slap his face. 'What right have you to talk to me like this?'

'Someone has to.' He caught hold of both wrists and forced her into the corner of her seat, holding her so tightly that she thought her bones would snap. 'Keep still and listen to me! We're not going home until you promise me you'll keep away from Christine's house in the evenings and you won't see her brother again.'

'Get lost!'

There followed a fraught five minutes in which she accused him of everything she could think of to accuse him with. She fought him physically, shouting hysterically until James was goaded into slapping her.

It stilled her and quietened her once and for all, and she glared at him mutinously, hating him, all the time he lectured her.

'You're fifteen years old, Debbie. Fifteen. But you're old enough to know what Dave wants from you, what would have happened if I hadn't found you tonight. He's been feeding you drugs and drink and the next thing on the agenda is sex. It's for this reason that I'm going to tell the Professor and your mother exactly what you were doing tonight. I'm leaving England in two weeks' time and I have to know that they're aware of the danger you're in. You won't give me your word to keep away from Chris and Dave, so you leave me no choice.'

He broke off, giving her the opportunity to change her mind. But Debbie didn't think he would stop her. She just couldn't believe he would be *that* rotten. 'You won't do that. They'll never let me out again if you do that.'

'They will. But they'll want to know exactly where you're going, and who with, and your deadline will be put back to something earlier than ten-thirty. Now the choice is yours. Look,' he went on, his voice softening considerably, 'I've told you before I'm aware of your unhappiness. You're just a child, mixed up and confused by all the changes in your life. I know you're upset about the divorce. But so is your mother, and your grandfather. And he's lost his wife recently. Don't you understand that he's still mourning? Don't you understand that, in a different way, your mother's mourning, too? You've given them nothing but cheek during the past few months and I'm not going to allow you to give them trouble of a practical nature. That's the last thing they need right now.

'And what do you think they're doing at this moment? They're waiting for me to find you, to bring you home. Your mother's in tears and your grandfather's terribly worried. Have a little consideration, Debbie. Grow up. Try talking to them instead of snapping at them. And find yourself some other friends from school—go swimming and bowling and riding in your spare time, like the nice girls do.'

'Nice girls? You're as big a snob as my mother! I hate that crummy school she sends me to. So does Chris.

Chris is the only one I get on with and I *won't* stop seeing her!'

He stopped her. He told Sir Henry and her mother everything, and they were horrified. Two weeks later, James left the country, and Debbie's freedom was severely curtailed. She was allowed out only on Friday and Saturday evenings—and she had to be home by eight o'clock.

Three months later, Christine Warwick was expelled from school for writing something vile about the headmistress on the lavatory walls. That, and other crimes.

Debbie didn't see Chris after her expulsion but she heard grapevine news about her. She heard about Chris's pregnancy when she was sixteen, about her shotgun wedding and her subsequent removal to London.

CHAPTER THREE

'YOU haven't forgiven me, have you? All this time, and you haven't forgiven me?'

Debbie was eighteen when James asked her this question. Three years had passed since she had seen him, three years during which he had been in San Francisco, and she had finished school and then she had begun a full-time secretarial course which she was now almost half way through.

It was October. James was spending a month in Europe, the first week of which he had spent at an international medical conference in Paris; the last three weeks he was spending at Vale House before starting work in Peru with the World Health Organisation.

'It isn't a question of forgiveness,' she answered. 'I would probably have straightened myself out, in time. I was fifteen, James. Most teenagers go through a wild phase, but they grow out of it. I didn't need your interference. Thanks to you, my movements were severely restricted after that episode with Dave Warwick. Gramps and my mother didn't really start to trust me fully until I left school.'

'Without my so-called interference,' he countered, 'you might have ended up like Christine Warwick—pregnant and obliged to marry someone you didn't love. There again you might have ended up as a drug addict. Who knows? It wasn't a chance I was prepared to take, and I think——'

'Oh, come off it!' she said impatiently.

'Well, you know what happened to Christine.'

'And how do *you* know about that?'

'Your grandfather told me in one of his letters.'

31

'And how did he know? He didn't hear it from me.'

James shrugged. 'Gossip, I suppose.'

Debbie clicked her tongue, flicking her eyes over him resentfully as he sat in the leather armchair near the fireplace, his long legs stretched out before him. 'Why didn't you go into town with Gramps and my mother?'

'Because I thought this would be an ideal opportunity to talk to you. Out there,' he said, grinning, 'is a wet Saturday afternoon. But in here,' the grin widened, 'is a nice warm fire, a pretty companion and the chance of a long and cosy chat.'

'You bore me, James. You always have and you always will.'

He just smiled. 'Do you still keep in touch with your father? How is he?'

'I write to him now and then,' she muttered. 'He's okay.' Deborah's father had remarried and was living in Canada now. She kept in touch with him, but she hadn't seen him since the divorce, and she never mentioned his name to her mother. Sometimes months passed when there was no contact, and Deborah accepted that her father was perfectly happy in his new life—a life which didn't include her.

'Good.' James looked at her, thoughtful. 'Well then, let's talk about something you find exciting—for instance, this boy who's coming to dinner tonight. How long have you been seeing him?'

'You know damn well how long I've been seeing Bob,' she said irritably. 'My grandfather will have told you all there is to know.'

'All? I doubt that very much.' This was said with blatant ambiguity, and she glared at him angrily.

James held up a hand. 'Don't get worked up, little Miss Firecracker. It was a simple question, wasn't it?'

'I've been seeing him for two months,' she said, her voice edged with impatience. 'We are unofficially engaged. Gramps has met him once, just before you got here. I know he doesn't like Bob, and Bob is well aware that he was invited here to dinner tonight so he can be given a thorough once-over. My mother and Gramps told me to invite him tonight—and that's as good as a royal command.'

'I hear he's a tennis coach at the club you belong to.'

'He's a tennis professional. He came to the club a few months ago and he's very popular and we're lucky to have him. And he isn't a boy, by the way. He's twenty.'

That was met with sarcasm. 'Oh. Excuse me. Anyway, it doesn't seem to have taken you long to fall in love with each other.'

'How long does it take?'

'How well do you know him, Debbie? Really?'

'Go to hell, James. I've had enough of your nosiness to last me a lifetime.' Deborah got up, picked up her book from the coffee table and went to sit on the window seat. She could easily have gone to her room to escape him but she didn't see why she should. This was her home, why should she have to spend the afternoon in her bedroom?

If it hadn't been pouring with rain, she'd have been spending the afternoon with Bob at the tennis club. She snapped the book closed, wondering what Bob was doing this afternoon. He wouldn't be teaching, not in this weather.

'I'm going for a walk.' She got up again, restless.

'In the rain?' James' voice was hardly more than a drawl, a sarcastic drawl.

She turned to look at him, her hands on her hips. 'I like walking in the rain. I trust that's okay with you?'

He looked her up and down, the dark brown eyes moving over her slowly, making her extremely uncomfortable. 'In some ways, at least, you have grown up since I last saw you.'

The remark brought an immediate flush to her cheeks, but James went on before she could make a suitable retort. 'How did you manage to get in to those jeans, Debbie? Let's hope the rain doesn't shrink them any further or you'll never be able to peel them off.'

She left the room without a word. He would be leaving on Wednesday, thank goodness. That meant she only had to put up with him for another four days.

Her thoughts switched to Bob as soon as she got outside. She was very much in love with him and she was seeing him three nights a week, on average. It wasn't enough, of course, but it was all he could manage due to his other commitments.

He usually dropped her off at the end of the drive when he brought her home after their dates. He had never asked to meet her family and Debbie hadn't encouraged his meeting them, knowing that her mother would not approve of him. But, a couple of weeks earlier, she had been asked by her mother to bring Bob in for a cup of coffee.

That had been an awkward, uncomfortable hour, more so for Bob than Debbie. Gramps and her mother had asked him dozens of questions and had made it quite obvious that he was under the magnifying glass for a preliminary examination.

She wished, now, that she had not mentioned their unofficial engagement. She should have waited until Bob could be more specific about when they would get married. But he was talking in terms of waiting for a couple of years until he was more established, until he had savings behind him.

Debbie sighed as she walked, venturing into the hills near Vale House. She looked forward so much to the day when she would have her own home, a home in which she would be mistress, in which she would bring up her children in an atmosphere that was always happy. She would never send them to boarding school and she would see that they never, ever, felt emotionally insecure. It would suit her, marriage and motherhood, she had no doubts at all about that.

She looked appreciatively at the vast expanse of greenery surrounding her, thinking that she must ask Bob exactly where they would live when they finally married. She hoped it would be here, in this vicinity, because it really was quite lovely living on the edge of the Peak District. Of course they would not be able to afford a home anything like the size of Vale House, but that didn't matter. What mattered was that it would be their home, her home, and she would decorate it and furnish it just as she wanted it to be.

Bob didn't come to dinner that night. When Debbie got back to the house, her mother and grandfather were home and she was told by Louise that Bob had just telephoned to say he couldn't come to dinner.

'But why?' Debbie was terribly disappointed at the idea of not seeing him.

'I'm afraid he wasn't too clear about that,' Louise said sceptically. 'He said there was someone he had to see, that he had to go away for the week-end. Anyway, I pointed out that he was giving us very short notice but I asked him to come on Monday evening.'

Deborah sighed inwardly. Her mother would interpret this cancellation as less than impeccable manners on Bob's part and she wouldn't take into account the probability of an emergency having cropped up in his life. 'It's probably something to do with his parents,' she pointed out defensively. 'I know his father isn't well. He's probably gone home to Stafford for the week-end.'

'I didn't ask, and he didn't say.'

'Have you got his parents' telephone number?' The question came from Gramps.

'No, I haven't.'

'You could get it from directory enquiries.'

She hesitated at her grandfather's suggestion. Bob

wouldn't like it if she rang him there. He might think she was checking up on him. He never liked it when she asked him what he'd been doing on the nights she didn't see him. 'I don't think there's any reason for me to do that, Gramps. I'm sure he'll have gone to Stafford. Besides, it's not for me to monitor his movements.'

'I shouldn't be too sure about that. I wouldn't trust him an inch if I were you.' Sir Henry was shaking his head. 'There's something about his attitude that's too cocky for my liking. I don't trust him.'

'Fortunately you don't have to.' As Debbie directed these words at her grandfather, she became aware of James' scrutiny. He was just watching, silent, in that awful way he had.

'He fancies himself too much,' Louise put in, fiddling with the flowers in a crystal vase on a side table. 'He's a good looking boy but he's only too well aware of it. And Bessie tells me you're not the only girl he's taking out. Are you aware of that, Deborah?'

'Bessie? Our Bessie?' What on earth did the housekeeper know about Bob? More gossip, no doubt. Why didn't people just mind their own business? *All* of them!

'I don't believe it,' she said coolly, addressing the room at large. 'If you'll excuse me, I'm going to take a bath.'

On Monday, Bob surprised Debbie by picking her up from secretarial college. She emerged from the building to see his sleek red sports car, and Bob was waving enthusiastically. He had been in Stafford; there was no mystery about where he'd spent the week-end.

He kissed her possessively as she got in his car, explaining everything, about his father being ill and asking to see him. 'I only got back an hour ago,' he said, pushing the light blond hair back from his forehead.

His positive green eyes were sparkling as he told her he'd missed her. 'I don't suppose we can get out of having dinner at your house, Deb? I'd like to take you out somewhere.'

'No,' she said dully, 'we can't. You'd really be in Mummy's bad books if you cancelled a second time! But it won't be too bad, and you needn't stay late. We can go out for a drive an hour after dinner's over.'

'Good. I'm not looking forward to being under your grandfather's microscope. It eats into my confidence.'

'Don't be silly!' She was genuinely surprised. 'Granted, he and Mummy are a bit obvious. But I can't imagine anything eating into your confidence. That's one thing I really admire about you, Bob.'

'Is that all?' He grinned, lifting her hand to his lips. 'Do you only admire one thing about me?'

'No. There are dozens of other things, but I've already told you about them!'

He drove her home and dropped her at the bottom of the drive, saying he'd be back when he was expected, namely seven-thirty.

Debbie went upstairs and bathed and dressed with care, dreading the next few hours but looking forward to being alone with Bob later on.

She stood by the window when she had finished dressing, looking at the October mist which was closing in on the house, and thinking about Bob. There were a couple of things she didn't understand about him, actually. Right at the start of their relationship they had fought because he was persistently getting fresh with her. Persistently and insistently. Their relationship had in fact almost finished before it was two weeks old. Bob was a very physical man, and it had been too much, too fast, for Debbie. She was eighteen and she had no experience at all. She also had no intention of making love with Bob. She had not forgotten what happened to

Christine and she was not on the pill because she saw
no reason why she should be.

She had told Bob plainly that he was wasting his
time, that if all he wanted was sex he could look
elsewhere and not bother taking her out again. He had
apologised, but on their very next date she had had to
fight him off again when he wanted to do more than
kiss her.

But that was the last time she'd had trouble with him.
After that, he had left her alone and had been content
with merely a goodnight kiss. Still, that was almost two
months ago, and Debbie was puzzled now because he
hadn't even attempted to touch her since then. She was
still of the same mind, and would draw the line if he
did, but human nature being what it is, she couldn't
held wondering why he found her so resistible!

The other thing which puzzled her was how he
managed to spend so much money on his car and his
clothes when he told her he was saving up. They
sometimes shared the bills when they went out, but Bob
always took her to nice places, different, out of the
ordinary places. He was just so exciting to be with!

The evening was not a disaster. Not until ten o'clock,
that was. After dinner, after a respectable length of time
had passed, she and Bob announced that they were going
out for a drive.

'I don't think so.' The words came from James in a
voice which was nothing less than vituperative. He had
just come back into the drawing room, having been
absent for a few minutes. 'Taking a drive is a very bad
idea, Debbie.'

She stared at him, barely able to contain the rush of
anger inside her. Ever since Bob had walked in to Vale
House, James had barely spoken a word. He had been
silent to the point of rudeness for hours—and now this!
And what business was it of his? Why did he seem to
think he had the right to interfere constantly in her life?

'What's that supposed to mean?' She snapped at him angrily, thoroughly sick of him.

James sat, accepting the glass of brandy Sir Henry handed to him. 'I mean it's thick with fog outside. A real pea-souper. I was just about to say that Bob will have to stay the night.'

'Is it really?' Sir Henry moved towards the windows but Debbie was already pulling back the heavy velvet curtains and looking out. It was absolutely dense, the type of fog in which one would be in danger walking, let alone driving.

Bob had no choice but to stay the night. Everyone realised that, and the evening continued even more stiltedly now that escape was impossible.

James made no contribution to the conversation whatsoever, Sir Henry nodded off briefly and Louise contented or discontented herself by asking Bob about his background and his parents.

It was with enormous relief that Debbie, and everyone else, retired for the night. Bob was shown to a guest room and Debbie closed the door on her own bedroom with a hasty prayer that the fog would be gone by morning.

She had been reading for almost an hour when there was a knock on her door. It was quiet, intended for her ears only, and she slipped out of bed knowing a feeling of panic and fear. Her room was at the end of the corridor and it was unlikely that anyone would know about her having a visitor, but what on earth was Bob thinking about in coming to see her? And how did he know which room was hers?

The door opened before she reached it, but it wasn't Bob. James Beaumont stepped inside, holding a finger to his lips.

'What the hell do you want? Get out!' Debbie reached automatically for her dressing-gown. She had hated him for his remark about her having grown up in some respects and she didn't want him scrutinising her further through her see-through nightie.

It was only when she had satisfactorily belted her dressing-gown around her that she looked at him properly. She lost colour when she looked at him, seeing instantly that he was here for a fight.

James was seething with anger. She knew the look only too well. His dark eyes were almost black with it, his square jawline was rigid with it and his mouth was compressed into a thin line.

'What now?' she demanded. 'What the devil's eating at you now?' Her anger was equal to his, equal if not greater.

'Keep your voice down. I don't want anyone else to hear what I've got to say to you.'

Debbie told him what to do with himself in no uncertain terms and instantly regretted her words when James advanced on her like an animal stalking its prey.

There was no fight. He took hold of her arm very tightly and moved it awkwardly so that a shaft of pain made her yelp like an injured puppy. He sat on her bed, forcing her to sit beside him.

'James, for God's sake! You're going to break my arm.'

'Not if you keep still,' he said quietly. 'Now then, I'm going to ask you a question and you're going to answer it. We can do this comfortably or we can do it uncomfortably. I haven't got time to play games, Debbie, so make up your mind.'

The pain seemed to be at her temples now, as well as in her arm. 'All right, all right! Ask what you want. Just let go of me!'

She stared at him as he let go of her. Never had she seen him quite like this before—not *this* angry! Without thinking about it, she realised she had better keep her temper in check.

Very clearly, very quietly, he said, 'Have you been to bed with Bob?'

She started, his audacity leaving her momentarily speechless. 'Why you——'

This time, the pain of his grip brought tears to her eyes and he held her so she could hardly breathe, let alone get up from the bed. 'Debbie, this is the last chance I'll have to talk to you in private. I'm leaving on Wednesday. Wouldn't it be easier for you to answer me than have me force it out of you?'

She nodded, her tawny eyes brilliant with tears and impotent fury. 'No, I haven't been to bed with him. And would you mind telling me what——'

'What business it is of mine? We're not using that old cry, are we?' He got to his feet, but she didn't move. 'I won't beat about the bush, Debbie. Do you know where I went today?'

She was rubbing her arm, thinking him quite mad. 'To see some of your doctor friends, wasn't it? To say hello before you leave England. A fine doctor you are! Do your friends go around dislocating——'

'Shut up and don't exaggerate. Can you remember exactly where I went today? I told you and the Professor at breakfast, remember?'

'I don't know. Some hospital in Leeds.'

'That's right.' He pushed his hands inside the pockets of his trousers. 'And you'll be astonished to learn that I saw Bob in the hospital. Yes, your Bob. Bob Hawthorne.'

'You're off your head.'

'To be more specific, Debbie, I was saying hello to an old colleague who's now working in the special clinic—and *that's* where I saw Bob. He was sitting in the waiting room, with his appointment card in his hand. In the waiting room of the special clinic.'

She stared at him stupidly. 'The special clinic? What's a special clinic?'

James looked heavenward. 'Good grief, don't you know anything? Are you just as idiotic and naïve as you were at fifteen? You're eighteen now and you don't even know——'

She shot to her feet as the penny dropped. 'You liar! You *liar*, James! Bob wasn't even in Leeds today, never mind the—that place.'

'Special clinic. Don't be afraid of saying it, Debbie. There is no stigma attached to special clinics, or the people who attend them. Most people who get sexual diseases are suffering mainly from bad luck. Of course with others it's a case of raging promiscuity. I wonder which it is with your Bob?'

'Neither! He wasn't in Leeds today. You're mistaken, I tell you!'

'I'm not mistaken.'

'Then you are lying.'

'Now why should I do that? Can you give me one good reason?'

'I—no. No, I can't. But you only met him tonight. How can you be sure it was him you saw today?'

'Because he's striking to look at with that mop of blond hair and he was wearing the clothes he had on tonight. And his clothes are rather flashy, to say the least!'

Debbie clamped her lips together, resisting that particular jibe. All sorts of things were going round in her head. But if this were true, why should Bob have gone to Leeds? Why not go to a clinic in Sheffield? So he wouldn't be seen by someone he knew, perhaps? No, James was wrong. He was being spiteful. He was telling lies, for some reason.

She got to her feet, looking at him from her inferior height. 'You wouldn't care to say this to Bob's face, would you?' She smiled smugly, knowing that this would put an end to the matter. James would have to admit the probability of mistaken identity now.

'I just have,' he said coolly. 'I've been talking to him in his room for the past twenty minutes.'

'What?'

'You heard me. He denied everything, of course. He said he'd spent the week-end and all day today with his sick father in Stafford.'

Debbie turned away from him. The humiliation was more than she could bear. To think that James had tackled Bob face to face about this!

'Listen, sweetheart.' James' voice was sickeningly gentle. 'What worries me as much as anything else is that your fiancé is a liar. If you'll answer a few more questions for me, I'll prove it to you. For example, he's just told me——'

'Get out of my room, James. I hate the sight of you.' She couldn't look at him. Tears were streaming down her face and she would not give him the satisfaction of seeing them.

He sighed. 'Very well. I am sorry, Debbie, but it's as well you should find out about his lying now, don't you think? Try asking him a few questions yourself, like who he sees on the nights when he isn't with you. Goodnight, Debbie.'

'Wait!' She sniffed, keeping her back to him. 'I—are you going to say anything about all this to——'

'No, not a word to anyone. I think you'll sort things out for yourself now.'

She did sort things out for herself—in time. Like the young fool that she was, she believed Bob when he insisted that James was mistaken. She joined with him in calling the older man everything nasty they could think of, and she was very easily persuaded by Bob that she should take his word rather than James'.

She continued seeing Bob for another month before the scandal finally broke, before it was known by every member of the tennis club that he was having an affair with a divorcée who was ten years his senior ... a wealthy divorcée who lived in Leeds. And there was more. He was also seeing a member of the tennis club whom Deborah had never met, a married woman whose husband turned up at the club one day and physically wiped the floor with Bob.

Bob left Yorkshire after that. Debbie left the tennis club and took up squash instead.

She never felt quite the same about men after her episode with Bob Hawthorne and it was two years before she even had a date with someone else.

CHAPTER FOUR

HAPPILY, James Beaumont had not been around to witness what a fool she had made of herself in her relationship with Philip Forster, but he did know about it. Gramps had written to him about her engagement, her *official* engagement, to Philip . . . and a subsequent letter had told of her being jilted.

Ever since her relationship with Philip had ended, Deborah had kept men and herself at an emotional distance. Experience had taught her that that was by far the safest thing to do. It was also a remarkably easy thing to do, not that she had become a man hater; Philip's let-down had not caused her to be maladjusted but it had taught her to be wary, very wary.

If there was one good thing that she could say for herself, it was that she learned from her past mistakes. She was of the firm opinion that people should learn from the past, and she had taken care to do just that.

But James didn't know this, and although she was now older and far from idiotic or naïve, he probably still thought of her as such. She would have to make him think otherwise if she were to live with him in harmony.

'. . . thanks to the delay,' he was saying now, still standing by the fireplace, one hand unconsciously rubbing his thigh as he talked, 'I only got two hours' sleep last night, and I must apologise for the whiskers.' He glanced from Sir Henry to the ladies. 'Still, there's plenty of time to bathe and shave before dinner, eh?'

'Don't worry about it, James!' Louise was all smiles, all enthusiasm. 'You look fine as you are!'

Sir Henry grunted. 'You've lost weight, about a

stone, I'd say. That's probably due to the climate you've been working in.' He looked James up and down with a professional eye. 'A few weeks here will put the beef back on you. How's the leg?'

'Fine. I'll stand for a while, though. It's stiff because I've been sitting in the car for so long.'

'I'd be interested to take a look at the wound,' Gramps went on, and Deborah sincerely hoped he didn't mean at this instant.

'Here we are!' Bessie came in with a tea tray. Short, plump, with hair which had always been grey, or so it seemed, she was the bustling type who appeared to have endless energy. 'A nice pot of tea for you, Dr Beaumont!' She put the tray down, beaming at him. 'Oh, it's so good to have you home!'

James' smile brought Deborah's eyes back to his face, to his mouth. 'What's all this "Dr Beaumont" business, Bessie? I've been James to you since I was seventeen, why is it different all of a sudden?'

The housekeeper opened her mouth to speak and promptly closed it again when she couldn't think of an answer. As she left the room, James' eyes followed her fondly, amusement dancing in their dark brown depths.

What had happened to him? He never used to smile so easily.

The following half hour was filled with scores of questions and answers as the latest news was generally caught up on. James drank his fill of the tea he had been gasping for and enquired after colleagues, friends and acquaintances.

'We could have a party next week!' Louise's eyes lit up as the inspiration came to her. 'A homecoming party, and we could invite everyone! Would you like that, James?'

Deborah watched him in the few seconds' pause before he answered Louise. He was registering how different she was, as well he might. Deborah's mother was a woman in love, but that was one item of news which hadn't been told to him yet.

'May I sleep on that one, Louise? At the moment I feel as if I've been transplanted from one world to another.'

'In other words,' said Sir Henry, 'he's exhausted. And it'll take some time for you to adjust to this new world, lad. Or rather, your old world.' He turned to Deborah.

'Debbie, take James upstairs and show him all the alterations we've had done up there. I hope he approves of his new rooms.'

She got to her feet, unable reasonably to refuse. It was at her suggestion that Vale House had been given a complete internal overhaul three years earlier. She had been mainly responsible for the decorating and carpeting which now graced the old house, for the installation of gas central heating to replace the old boiler system. But all she had done was to make the home more comfortable and colourful, in a taste which was right for it. There had been no radical changes; that was something she would never want to make to the house she loved so much. The furniture, much of which consisted of antique pieces, was just as it had always been, apart from a few additions which were mostly in the bedrooms.

As soon as she and James got into the hall, he said, 'I thought you told me you much preferred to be called by your full name these days? Henry still calls you Debbie.'

She inclined her head. 'Gramps is too old to start changing his habits.'

'I'll have difficulty myself. I can't think of you as anything other than Debbie.'

This was precisely what she wanted him to do. The Debbie, the young girl he had known, had gone. 'Then please make an effort.'

He bowed slightly, picking up his suitcases so she couldn't see his eyes. Were they full of amusement again?

She picked up the third and smallest suitcase and a tattered canvas hold-all. 'Are these all your possessions?'

He walked upstairs ahead of her. 'Every material thing that I own in the world. I'm going to have to buy some new clothes pronto. And a car. Does Henry's old Humber still go? I know he's still got it, but he can't use it now—since his stroke.'

'He's kept you very up-to-date with his letters, hasn't he? Nobody's tried to start the Humber for ages. I don't know whether it'll work or not. I think Gramps is keeping it for posterity . . . This way, James.'

He turned as he reached the landing, frowning.

'We've all had a change-round,' she explained. 'I'm using what used to be the master bedroom. Your rooms overlook the back of the house now. There's an en suite bathroom which used to be a guest room. I'm sure you'll like it.'

'I'm sure I will.'

They put his cases at the foot of his bed and Deborah showed him everything there was to see upstairs, including her own rooms. She heard, without interest, his noises of approval as he looked around her immaculate bedroom and bathroom, both of which had been decorated with soft, warm shades of pink and beige.

'Thank you.' She said this in an automatic response to his compliments on her taste.

His eyes moved slowly over her face, over the smart, emerald green suit she was wearing and on to her court shoes. It was done slowly, very slowly. Deborah felt herself bristle. 'Why the scrutiny?'

'Why not?' he reasoned. 'It's seven years since I've seen you. Your taste in clothes has certainly changed.'

She looked him over likewise, her voice neutral as she spoke. 'I could say the same about you.'

'You may say the same about me,' he smiled.

She shrugged, turning for the door, but James caught hold of her wrist. 'You hardly spoke downstairs, I could smell resentment in the air. I still can.'

'Don't be silly.'

His eyes narrowed. 'Surely you don't still hate me? After all these years?'

'Of course not. I never—No,' she faltered, 'that's not true. I used to hate you.'

'Have you never considered that I might have done you a few favours in the past?'

'Of course I've considered it, James. I'm twenty-five years old now, I don't view things with the eyes of a fifteen-year-old or even an eighteen-year-old.'

'But?'

'But I never liked your *methods* of interfering. I still don't think of them kindly.'

'I tried to fight your obstinacy with reason but it didn't work, so your temper I fought with temper. That was the only way I could get through to the fiery little redhead that you were . . . are.'

'*Were.* You were right the first time.' She gave him the cool smile. 'But don't let's dredge up the past. I'll see you later.'

It was during the pre-dinner drinks, the champagne with which they were celebrating James' homecoming, that he was told the remaining and most significant piece of family news.

Comfortable in his arm chair, Sir Henry looked curiously at his daughter and shook his head slightly. 'Well, Louise, I've been wondering when you're going to tell James what else has been happening around here?'

'I——' Louise got no further than that. Her father had taken over.

'There are wedding bells in the air. What do you think of that?' He gave James a broad wink.

James' eyes went instantly to Deborah, who was

sitting at some distance from him. '*Really?* I had no idea, Debbie. This must have happened recently.'

'I am not,' she said clearly, 'the person concerned.' She had imagined what he had been wondering ... 'And who is it this time?' She could almost see the question in his eyes.

'Daddy!' Louise protested. 'You can't make a statement like that! You shouldn't, it's just not true.'

Sir Henry simply smiled.

'Louise? *You're* getting married? Why, that's wonderful news, wonderful! Who's the lucky man?' James was genuinely pleased for her.

Louise held up a hand, smiling through her slight embarrassment. At forty-nine she was still a very attractive woman, taller than Deborah but with a similar shade of hair. 'You'll meet him tomorrow, James, he's coming to dinner. He has *not* proposed to me, but I've been seeing him regularly for the last few months. I was introduced to him at a party in early December and—well, we get on like a house on fire!'

James smiled. 'What does he do?'

'He's an academic. He's Dutch, he's over here on a sabbatical year and he's spent most of his time travelling round Lancashire, Yorkshire and Derbyshire visiting stately homes, old buildings, castles, ruins and the like.' She laughed softly, her admiration for Hans Bakker evident in her eyes. 'I've been astonished by how many of these things there are in the industrial north! *I've* been astonished, and I'm a native! But Hans has taken me to places of interest which I didn't know existed. He really is a quite remarkable man and ... I'm sure you'll like him.' Louise finished on a quiet note, unwilling to enthuse too much.

James nodded, encouraging her to go on. 'I look forward to meeting him. Tell me more, Louise.'

'Well, he's one year younger than I, he's a widower and he hasn't got any children. He's going back to

Amsterdam in the middle of May and he's invited me to go with him, to show me some of the sights.'

'To see whether she likes the place,' Sir Henry amended chuckling. 'And to see how she likes the house she'll be living in when they're married. That's what it's all about, really, make no mistake. Hans has almost said as much.'

'Almost, only almost.'

'I don't think there's any need to ask you whether you'd accept a proposal from him,' James smiled. 'Does the idea of living in Holland appeal to you?"

'Yes. As you know, I spent many years living abroad with Deborah's father. Of course we never lived in Holland, but I once spent ten days there on holiday. Yes, I'm sure I'd like it.'

Deborah listened and watched with interest. It saddened her that her relationship with her mother was not a particularly close one. It never had been. She loved her dearly, of course, but the simple truth was that basically they had nothing in common. She was not unlike her mother to look at and she had inherited her natural grace of movement, had acquired some of her refinements; they shared a similar taste in clothes and material things of quality but their way of thinking was totally different.

Louise had never had a job as such. Over the years they had lived at Vale House she had become more and more involved with fund-raising projects for various charities and committees of one sort or another. She was also artistic and painted rather well in an amateur capacity, going out regularly on painting sessions with the local art club when the weather permitted it.

That her mother would be married to Hans Bakker in the not too distant future, Deborah had no doubt at all. She only hoped that things would work out well for her, she hoped very much that that would be the case.

'And how do you get on with Hans?' James asked. 'Do you like him, Debbie?'

Debbie. What a short memory he had. She let it pass though, answering his questions with thought. 'I like him, yes, and he's very pleasant and sweet to me. But my mother's being happy with him hardly depends on my opinion of him. Their marriage is hardly my business, I just hope it works out well.'

James considered her words for several seconds, his dark eyes looking deep inside her as he listened, then considered.

Deborah broke the eye-contact, becoming aware that her grandfather's attention was shifting from her to James and back to her. She wondered what he was thinking. She wondered what James was thinking, too.

She found out what James was thinking. 'Do you see any reason why things shouldn't work out well for your mother?'

The question came smoothly and Deborah answered it truthfully. 'There are no reasons that I can see. I just think that—well, once bitten, twice shy. Mummy should think carefully.'

'I'm sure she has,' he said, frowning for some reason.

They were half way through dinner before Deborah became aware of how much thought she was giving to James. It didn't show, but her attention was on him constantly. He was sitting opposite her at the dining table, and the conversation between the other three was non-stop as the years between James' last visit were filled in in some detail.

She had by no means made up her mind about him. He was still a stranger who was not a stranger, to a large extent an unknown quantity. He talked about his work and his working conditions, latterly in Africa, about the local uprising during which he had been shot, about the poverty, the lack of facilities there. At one point he had worked on a compound which was actually in a clearing in the jungle and he talked of the natives who had been his patients there, of their fears and superstitions.

That James had led a very colourful and interesting life for the past few years was obvious. It had also been a hard life, a spartan life without luxuries or comforts and he had lived it by choice. He could have stayed in America, where he would have earned more money and worked with the latest technology in the finest hospitals.

But he had chosen not to, and his work in Africa and other countries had given him experiences and a form of education which had caused a fundamental change in him. Quite what that change was, Deborah still could not define because there were too many conflicting impressions. There was, for instance, a relaxation about him which never used to be there, it was as if he were ... as if he were deeply, inwardly content. Yet there was also an alertness, a vitality both mental and physical which Deborah had never noticed before.

Adding these things up, she certainly did not have the overall impression of a man who was tired, but when Gramps suggested to James that he take a long break from work, the younger man confirmed that that was his intention.

'You haven't had a holiday since the last time you were here, James. In fact, if I add up the time you've taken off during the last ten years, it would amount to—what? Six weeks?'

'The last ten years have been good ones, Henry. I wouldn't change a thing about them—well, except for the odd bullet here and there!'

Sir Henry's bushy eyebrows came down and almost met across the bridge of his nose. James was being given a thorough scrutiny, and *his* eyebrows went up in amusement. 'What's the verdict, Professor?'

'Six months, James. Lay off for six months. You've earned it. I think you need it, too.'

James threw back his head, his laughter deep and attractive. 'I'll settle for three, Henry.'

'Done!' Gramps was laughing now, leaning forward to slap James heartily on the back. 'That's about all I could hope for!'

The old man and the young man were enjoying themselves, enjoying each other, and Deborah watched the interplay with feelings which were very ambivalent. She didn't want James here, but she enjoyed what he gave to, what he did for, her grandfather. James Beaumont was the son Sir Henry had never had. And in those few moments, James' love and respect for Sir Henry was unmistakable. This pleased Deborah no end because in that respect, at least, she and James had something in common.

She sighed inwardly, knowing a sense of shame because it was selfish of her to wish James elsewhere. It was selfish and it was probably silly, too. What difference would his presence in the house make to her, really? But it does, she argued with herself. It's already making a difference. Why, why does this man have the knack of making me feel self-conscious even now? So much water has gone under the bridge of my life and yet I *still* feel self-conscious in his company, despite my determination not to!

She looked up to find that his eyes were on her. 'You're not saying much, Debbie—Deborah. Tell me what's been happening to you lately. How's business?'

'Accelerating. It gets busier during the summer months.'

'Do you stay open all year round?'

'No, from March to December. Experience has shown me that it isn't worth opening during January and February.'

'And when am I going to be invited to see your shop?' he asked.

She shrugged carelessly. 'Any time.'

They all went back to the drawing room when Bessie announced that coffee had been put in there for them. A little later, Gramps opened the bottle of rare old Scotch and raised his glass in yet another toast to James. 'Welcome home, my boy! I'm glad you came back when you did. If you'd left it two or three years longer, I might not have been around when you got here.'

'Gramps!' Deborah was horrified, and it was so unlike her grandfather to say something negative like that.

James laughed it off. 'Are you thinking of going somewhere, Henry?'

'Not just yet, but no one lives for ever.'

'Gramps——'

'Come off it, Henry. You'll get a telegram from the Queen, and we all know it.' He glanced at Deborah.

Gramps was laughing too, now, but she wished he wouldn't talk like that. He never had before.

In the drawing room there was a huge aquarium which had been around as long as Deborah could remember. Over the past few years two more had been installed in the house, one of which was in the conservatory, and James was now urged to inspect Gramps' Red Sea Rainbow Butterfly fish. Difficult to obtain in England and very difficult to look after according to Gramps, these tropical fish were his newest acquisition and his pride and joy.

CHAPTER FIVE

'HE hasn't changed at all, has he?' The statement came from Gramps and it was said with satisfaction.

Neither James nor Louise had come down to breakfast yet, the former was probably sleeping off the effects of jet-lag and it was a little too early for Louise to be up and around . . . when she didn't have an outing planned with Hans.

Deborah almost always had breakfast alone with Gramps in the conservatory, in which there were lots of plants and a cold-water aquarium. He would see to his fish, then he and Deborah would have a typically English breakfast and a chat. This morning, of course, James was the topic of conversation. Already she was sick of hearing his name; it was James this and James that. And it was no different with Bessie; she had begun the day by telling Deborah that James would be sleeping late this morning—and she had gone on to enthuse over attributes which Deborah just could not see in him.

'You think not?' She looked at her grandfather in surprise. 'But he's not half as serious and sullen as he used to be.'

'Sullen?' It was as if Sir Henry didn't know the meaning of the word. 'James was never sullen!'

Deborah let it pass. She didn't want to encourage this conversation. For the first time in many years she actually found herself wanting to get away from her grandfather when, twenty minutes later, he was still talking about the wretched James. She consoled herself with the knowledge that it wouldn't always be like this, not once the novelty of his homecoming had worn off.

Still, she was glad to get out of the house that first morning. Joan would cheer her up, and maybe she'd like to go out somewhere tonight? Deborah would certainly like to, she had done her duty by spending the previous evening at home and while she didn't go out often, she felt very much like making an escape tonight.

Joan Clegg had worked for Deborah for the past two years. Since she had worked in the county library from the day she left school, Deborah had known her by sight for a long time and she had been astonished when Joan answered an advertisement for an assistant which Deborah had put in the local newspaper.

Deborah hadn't really expected to find someone who knew about antiques, and this was the case with Joan. But that had been two years ago and Joan now knew as much about the business as her boss did, if not more. She was a clever woman, who was enthusiastic and the two of them had become fast friends. She was ten years older than Deborah and she had an extremely dry, often wicked sense of humour which Deborah loved. Unfortunately, much of Joan's humour was directed against herself. She was six feet one and a half inches tall and terribly self-conscious about it.

Deborah's shop premises once used to be a workman's cottage and it stood, detached, on what was now a main road several miles from Vale House. She depended largely on passing trade and, in the summer months, there was no shortage of that since foreigners and Britons alike came in abundance to the Peak District. She parked her car on the patch of waste ground at the side of her shop, carefully lifting her box of goodies from the back seat. She had done well at the auction yesterday, having acquired several pieces of antique jewellery and two pill-boxes for which she already had a buyer—a local person.

Busy with a duster, Joan peered at her over the top of the spectacles which were usually half way down her nose and which gave her an owl-like appearance. She always got to the shop first and had a dust round before opening time. She really was a gem. ''Morning, Deborah! What's up? You don't look at all pleased with yourself.'

'There's nothing wrong with me.' Deborah put the box on the small counter in the corner. 'It's our—lodger. The fatted calf was trotted out last night and I am *sick* of hearing his name!'

Joan gulped exaggeratedly. 'I'd better not use it then. But—you don't find him any different?'

'He's considerably different, yet somehow he manages to be just as irritating as he used to be. I can't quite work out why.'

That James was coming home, Deborah had naturally told her friend, but she hadn't gone in to great detail about the past, just enough to let Joan know how she felt about Sir Henry's surrogate son.

'When do I get to meet him?' Joan wanted to know.

'When he comes poking his nose around here!' She waved her arms about in agitation. 'And that's the end of the subject of Dr Beaumont. What are you doing tonight?'

Joan blinked in surprise. 'Er—I'm going out with a seven foot Swede who's got more money than sense.'

'Now, what are you really doing tonight?' Deborah grinned.

'Well, I'll tell you,' she patted the silky brown hair which just hung at the side of her face. It was dead straight, with a fringe, it almost reached her shoulders and it was quite the wrong style for her thin face. 'I thought I'd stay in and wash this.'

Deborah thought she meant it; it wouldn't have been unusual, and most of Joan's witticisms were delivered with a deadpan face. 'Then how about going to the pictures with me?'

'Oh, I'm sorry, Deborah, I really am going out

tonight. Not with a seven foot Swede, alas—not with anyone, in fact, unless you count Frank. We said we'd go to my sister's for dinner. It's her birthday.'

Frank was her fifty-year-old brother with whom she lived. He was a bachelor and she was a spinster; she was a book worm and he spent most of his evenings playing with his home computer. Neither of them had an exciting existence but neither of them did anything about it—though Joan was always threatening to. Every morning, when they had coffee, she would pore over the lonely hearts ads in the Sheffield newspaper and vow that one of these days she would answer some of them. She was, she said, just working up the courage to do it.

'Bother.' Deborah clicked her tongue, thinking. 'Then I'll ring Denis. Perhaps he'd like to go out tonight.'

Joan looked heavenward, stuck her hands on her bony hips and sighed with impatience. 'I can't understand why you bother with him. If I looked like you look I'd be listed in the little black book of two hundred men who were itching to take me out—but Denis Brown would not be one of them, poor devil. He's as old as sin compared to you, and as original as yesterday's news. Even *I* wouldn't have him,' she finished, rolling her eyes. 'Well, maybe at a pinch . . .'

Deborah just smiled. Neither Joan nor anyone else understood her relationship with Denis Brown and she made no attempt to enlighten people. Her arrangement with him suited them both right down to the ground, and it had nothing whatever to do with romance.

She phoned him and fixed a date for that evening, then she phoned home and told Bessie she would not be in to dinner, that she was going out straight from work.

While her evening was taken care of, her day did not go as peacefully as she had expected. At lunch time she drove into town because there was a sale on in her favourite lingerie shop and today was the last day for reductions. On returning to work she discovered that James had called in—already. And Joan forgot all about her promise not to mention his name.

'Well, it didn't take him long, did it?' This was Deborah's response to the news of James' visit. 'How did he get here? Was he in an old Humber, by any chance?'

Joan shook her head. 'He wasn't wearing a hat.'

The younger girl couldn't help laughing. 'All right, all right—what did he have to say?'

Joan's eyes twinkled mischievously. They were her best feature and really quite lovely. 'He was in your mother's car, but I didn't realise that until he drove away—and I stood at the window and watched him. You might have warned me, Deborah, you might have warned me!'

'About what? Was he funny with you?'

'Funny? He was charm personified! At first I thought he was a customer so I was charming, too, even more so than usual because—well, he is *gorgeous*! You might have told me how attractive he is!'

Deborah shrugged. 'He hasn't always been that good looking. And in any case——'

'And I never dreamt he was a Yorkshireman, what with his mid-Atlantic accent and that—I don't know—that *air* about him!'

'He never used to speak so——'

'Deborah, don't keep telling me about what he used to be. All I know is that he's charming, he's got the most attractive suntan, a chiselled and classically handsome face, a superbly muscular physique and——'

'Joan, I think I'm going to be sick. Have you finished?'

'*And* he's half an inch taller than I am. So I can honestly tell you that we saw eye to eye.'

'Just tell me what he wanted, will you?'

Joan looked disappointed at having her enthusiasm stopped like this. 'He thought you'd be here to show him around. I hope you don't mind, but I did that, showed him what there is upstairs and everything.'

'I'm delighted. You've saved me the bother.'

'Then I gave him a cup of coffee and delayed him a bit because I thought you might be back any minute and——'

'You didn't! When you know what I think of him?'

'No, I didn't.' Joan's square shoulders lifted in a shrug. 'I gave him a cup of coffee and delayed him because there was no one in the shop and I really enjoyed talking to him. You never mentioned that his main interest is in paediatrics, that he specialises in——'

'Anyone less likely to be a good children's doctor, I cannot imagine!' Deborah interrupted impatiently.

Her assistant was frowning. 'You've really got it in for him, haven't you? Why, Deborah?' She was serious now, very much so.

Deborah waved a dismissive arm. 'I just don't like him, that's all. I simply do not like the man.'

Whatever Joan had been about to say—or ask—next, she changed her mind. After a momentary hesitation she said, 'Anyway, he said he was going shopping for some new clothes. When I told him that that's what you were doing, he said what a pity it was that he'd missed you because you could have taken the afternoon off and the two of you could have shopped together.'

'Taken the afternoon——' Deborah was irritated at his presumption. Without realising she was thinking aloud, she said, 'Oh, yes! That's all I need—James Beaumont going with me while I shop for my undies!'

'It might have been fun,' Joan offered, the twinkle back in her eye.

For an hour after closing time Deborah stayed in the shop, alone, sitting by the window and just letting her mind wander, about nothing in particular. She had an hour to kill before it was time to meet Denis.

It was the first week of May and the nights were getting longer. It was still quite light outside but the moon was clearly visible. It was also nearly full. Deborah looked up at it, knowing a sudden feeling of loneliness even while she was glad of the silence surrounding her.

Two days. James had not been at Vale House for two full days when history started to repeat itself.

When Deborah went down to breakfast the next morning, she found James in the conservatory, sitting alone at the breakfast table. From the windows she could see her grandfather outside, talking to the gardener.

'Good morning, Deborah.' He greeted her with a smile which softened the intensity of his dark brown eyes. 'Cold this morning, isn't it?'

In was in that instant that she began to realise what was different about him. It was in his eyes. There was about them a warmth and humour which was new, the impression that they could look right inside her which was not new, and there was ... yes, something which she now recognised as wisdom. This was new, this look which she could only define as wisdom. She could see it in abundance in her grandfather's eyes but she had never noticed it in James' before. It hadn't been there before. Maybe he had grown more tolerant, more mellow, now he was older? It was to be hoped so.

She looked away, irritated with herself for her scrutiny of him. He really was a good looking man, she had to admit, and the white polo neck sweater he was wearing made a striking contrast against the darkness of his skin. If he really was in need of a rest, it certainly didn't show. There was a crackling vitality about him which seemed to fill the room. 'I wouldn't know whether it's cold or not, I haven't been outside yet.'

Bessie came in as he answered her, armed with two

plates of bacon and eggs. 'Well,' he said, 'I'm very glad of the central heating. I had the radiator on full blast in my room last night.'

'You've been used to sleeping in the tropics,' Bessie put in, smiling indulgently. 'Sir Henry said you shouldn't wait for him,' she went on, putting their breakfasts before them, 'he's discussing the rose garden with Mr Ollerenshaw.'

Alone again, James talked for a while about Deborah's shop. He seemed genuinely interested and she responded very pleasantly. Besides, for her grandfather's sake she had to make an effort at friendliness with James.

'No, I don't do much in the way of furniture, but it isn't a question of capital, it's a question of space. I simply haven't got room to keep much furniture, not larger pieces, anyway.'

He nodded, putting his knife and fork together as he finished clearing his plate. 'Yes, of course. I should've realised. Besides, finance wouldn't present a problem to you, would it?'

Deborah thought he was referring to her inheritance, the money she had got when she reached twenty-five. James probably knew about that, didn't he? Her grandfather told him *everything*. 'No, within reason.'

But James was not referring to her grandmother's money. His all-seeing eyes met and held hers, and he said, 'Quite. It must be handy having a boy friend who is also your bank manager.'

Her eyes flashed impatiently at the tone he had used. His sarcasm had been mild—but it was there. 'He is not my boy friend.'

'Perhaps that was the wrong description.' He shrugged casually. 'But what else can I refer to him as? Tell me, what do you call a man who's dating a girl young enough to be his daughter?'

Deborah silently counted to ten. She had to. The way

he let his question hang in the air infuriated her but she would *not* lose her cool. She had reached number seven when he went on in an apparently casual and conversational tone.

'So you now have a predilection for older men, Debbie? Denis Brown must be—what? Twenty years your senior?'

She put a smile on her face. 'Twenty-two, actually. He's forty-seven.'

'And how do you get on with his two teenage sons?'

She ignored that. 'I take it you know Denis?'

'I knew him years ago, before his wife died, when he was assistant manager in Wakefield. His managing the main Sheffield branch must be quite a feather in his cap.'

'He worked for his promotion.' The tension in her voice was audible to her own ears, and anger had started to simmer inside her.

'You were with him last night, weren't you? When Bessie gave us the message about your going out for the evening, Henry guessed it would be Denis you were with.'

Deborah put her hands flat on the surface of the table. 'Yes,' she said stiffly, her tawny eyes looking at him with hatred. 'And you are poking your nose into my affairs—again!'

'Affairs? You're having an affair with him? I thought you just said he wasn't——'

'Damn you, James, it was a figure of speech! I meant that you're poking your nose into my business, my life. *Again!*'

He blinked in surprise, his dark eyes looking innocent, supposedly innocent, and she wanted to slap him. 'Why, Debbie, we're just chatting, that's all. I'm still catching up on the news. You see, there'd been no mention in Henry's letters of a man in your life, not since your fiancé, in fact, and I just wondered——'

'Well, don't!' She raised her voice, shoving her plate away before she had quite finished, too angry to eat any more. 'If you *must* live in this house, kindly leave me alone and don't ask questions which are none——'

'Good morning.'

She turned to see Gramps standing in the doorway, staring at her with a mixture of anger and disappointment, but it was the latter which affected her most. Hell, he had obviously heard what she'd just said to his beloved James. 'Gramps . . . Good morning, Gramps.' She blushed furiously, looking down at the table cloth.

'There's a phone call for you, James. It's a lady, Dr Ann Shepherd calling from Johannesburg.'

James thanked him and left the room.

Deborah faced her grandfather.

'What was all that about?' Sir Henry sat down, his expression grave.

'Gramps, I will not allow him——'

'Just answer the question, please. I want to know what prompted that remark about him living here.'

Deborah sat back in her chair, sighing. She would tell him everything and let him see for himself what a nerve James Beaumont had. 'Firstly he implied that there's something distasteful in my going out with Denis Brown. He seems to think he's my sugar daddy or something.'

'Now how could he possibly think that?'

'I don't know! He asked me whether I was having an affair with him. How's that for audacity?'

Gramps looked at her blankly. 'What's audacious about that?'

'Don't throw the question back at me,' she said firmly, disgusted. 'Just answer me this—how would *he* like it if I gave him the third degree about the women in his life?'

Sir Henry answered her very patiently, his good arm reaching over to pat her hand. 'Calm down, love. You and James have known each other many years, after all. It's perfectly reasonable that he's interested in what happens to you, Debbie. It isn't nosiness or interference, it's just friendly interest.'

At the sound of James' returning footsteps, she clamped her lips together. An idea had just struck her, a way of showing her grandfather that what was permissible for James was permissible for her, too.

She turned to James, smiling, as he sat down at the breakfast table. 'More tea, James?'

'Thank you.'

She poured tea for all of them, then asked, in a tone of 'friendly interest', whether Ann Shepherd was someone he'd met in Africa.

'Yes, we worked together for the past year. She went back to Johannesburg on the day I left for England. She's a super girl and a very good doctor.'

'Girl?'

'Well, she's twenty-nine,' he smiled.

'Is she single?'

'Oh, indeed, and that's how she intends to stay.' James' answers came easily to questions he seemed not to mind in the least. But he would, he would!

'She told you that, did she?'

His black brows went up briefly. 'You get to know someone very well when you work with them in the middle of nowhere for twelve months.'

'And why was she ringing you just now?'

'To see that I got home all right. Sweet of her, wasn't it?'

Deborah gave him her softest smile, a genuine one because her thoughts were quite amusing. 'Perhaps she fell in love with you, out there in the depths of the African jungle?'

His eyes started laughing at her. 'Who knows?'

She put her next question bluntly. 'Was she your lover?'

The amusement left his eyes and she knew a sense of triumph. No, he didn't like it. Not one bit. He thought for a long moment before answering, glancing at Sir Henry before moving his eyes back to hers. 'You know,' he said quietly, 'this probably has something to do with the male ego, but I'd rather say I was her lover. But yes, we were lovers. Our affair started four months after she came to the hospital and it finished on the day we left . . .'

Sir Henry started laughing even before James finished talking. '. . . Professionally speaking, this is off the record. Of course I don't mind telling you, Debbie, since I can trust you and we've known each other so well for so long.'

To the rumble of her grandfather's laughter and the silent laughter dancing in the younger man's eyes, Deborah stood up and excused herself.

She got into her car and drove away from the house with tears of frustration stinging her eyes. Damn James Beaumont. Damn him, *damn* him!

She did not go out with Denis that evening, she went to his home and spent the evening watching television with him. Never before had they spent two consecutive evenings together, and they had never spent an evening watching television. But Deborah simply did not want to go home that evening.

The point she had failed to prove over breakfast had still left the taste of humiliation in her mouth when it was closing time at the shop. That her grandfather had taken James' side in the issue had made her wonder, briefly, whether she was in fact being too much on the defensive with James. She had given this some thought during the course of the day but she had decided no, she wasn't being too defensive. With him, she couldn't be too defensive! Besides, Gramps didn't know about James' cruelty to her in the past, about what an interfering, brutal swine he had been.

So she phoned Denis Brown and invited herself over to his house. He was delighted; he cooked dinner for her and his seventeen year old son, whose brother was away at university, and when the boy later went out, she and Denis settled in front of the box.

Their relationship was based on mutual . . . use. Use rather than need. She had got to know him a little when, three years earlier, she had been opening her shop and had applied to him for a bank loan to help her do it. She didn't have her inheritance then, and she did not want to borrow money from her grandfather or her mother because she wanted to start a business entirely under her own steam and the fact that the bank had confidence in her helped her own confidence enormously. She did not want special favours from her family, or any financial responsibility towards them, although she did have to obtain the signature of a guarantor for the loan and Sir Henry had been the only one she could ask. Still, she had long since repaid her debt to the bank.

At the time of her original business with the bank manager, Denis had been widowed for two or three years. Deborah had asked him out to lunch by way of saying thank you—and had found him quite a different man once he was outside the old-established, respectable premises which were his place of work. Outside his own domain he lacked confidence. She saw his loneliness, even though their first social conversation did not venture on to personal matters.

A whole year went by and then one day he called into the shop, looking for a gift for someone. One thing led to another and he happened to tell Deborah that he had two complimentary tickets to a show at the Palace Theatre in Manchester. He had no one to go with; she liked the theatre—and that resulted in their first date.

Since then they had gone out together on average

once a month. They went mainly to the theatre, the enjoyment of which was something they had in common, always having a meal out either before or after the show, and on several occasions Deborah had acted as hostess for him in his home when he had had company he was obliged to entertain.

That was all there was to it. Mutual use. It suited both of them to have someone with whom they could go out to see something they each enjoyed. But Deborah had got to know Denis far better than he had got to know her. He was still very much in love with the memory of his wife, while Deborah ... well, as far as Deborah was concerned, Denis was *safe* to be with. He wanted absolutely nothing from her and he never questioned her as to why she didn't have a relationship with, or at least occasionally go out with, men of her own age. Nor did she ever volunteer this information. That her final disenchantment with men had been brought about by her being jilted by Philip Forster was something only she need be concerned about. She was not a man-hater; she just didn't want to get emotionally involved with one ever again.

It was turned one o'clock when she got home that night. Denis lived on the other side of Sheffield and his home was almost an hour's drive from Vale House. She let herself in, surprised to find that Hans Bakker's car and several others were parked outside the house. So her mother and Hans had stayed at home this evening and, by the sound of it, there had been something of a dinner party.

Laughter, voices were coming from the drawing room, and Deborah paused in the hall, debating whether to go in and wish everyone goodnight. Among the voices she could recognise that of her grandfather's general practitioner, and that of his solicitor and his wife.

She got to the bottom of the stairs, deciding not to

bother with pleasantries; she didn't want to get drawn into conversation.

'Deborah?'

She turned to see her mother coming from the kitchen, a jug of water in her hand. 'Hello, Mummy. So James decided to have a party, after all, did he?'

'Not at all! He told me this morning he'd rather not.' Louise laughed, waving an arm in the direction of the drawing room. 'This is quite impromptu! Max and Sophie called this afternoon, to say hello to James, and ended up being invited to stay for dinner. Hans came at six, as expected, and the other three just happened to call after dinner and, oh, well!'

Deborah smiled. Her mother seemed happy with the way things had turned out. There was never a shortage of visitors at Vale House. Sir Henry was very well liked and people called in to see him any time it took their fancy—which he loved. 'It sounds as if you've all had a good time, but I won't bother saying goodnight. I'm quite tired.'

'Oh, I wanted to—never mind,' Louise glanced at the water in her hand. 'I'll just take this in and then I'll pop up and see you, darling. There's something I want to ask you about. Give me five minutes.'

Deborah kicked her shoes off the instant she got into her room, sitting down at her dressing table to take the pins from her hair and allow it the freedom she always prevented it from having. When loose, it was too curly and wild for her liking. The trouble was that there was too much of it. Still, she mused, lightly massaging her scalp, it had calmed down quite a lot compared to the way it used to be. It used to be very curly and a lot redder than it was now, just a mop of hair she couldn't do anything with. These days it was manageable because it was longer and could be worn in a knot, and the colour had mellowed of its own accord to a reddish-auburn which was quite attractive. Even she thought so.

Debating whether or not to take a bath, she hung her dress in the wardrobe, automatically saying 'Come in' when her mother knocked on her door.

But it wasn't her mother she had invited in.

Deborah turned and froze, deep colour flooding her cheeks at the sight of James Beaumont.

He was half way through a sentence before his eyes located her on the other side of the room, by the wardrobe. 'Deborah, I wanted to——'

He stopped dead, his eyes absorbing every detail of her appearance before she could do anything about covering herself. She was wearing the half-cup bra she had bought in the sale the previous day, matching panties which were equally brief, a white, lacy suspender belt which completed the set and very sheer, smoky grey stockings.

They looked at each other. James' eyes went down the length of her body and returned slowly to meet her horrified stare. She didn't move and he didn't apologise for his intrusion. They just looked at each other for several seconds before his eyes started roving again and Deborah snapped into action, reaching swiftly for her négligé. 'Do you *mind*, James?'

'Not in the least,' he drawled. 'I haven't seen anything so deliciously provocative in a long time.' His eyes moved back to hers. 'But tell me, for whose benefit is all this feminine satin and lace? Denis Brown's? I doubt it. Do you know what I think, *Deborah*? I think I've had a glimpse of the woman you try so desperately to hide.'

'. . . the woman you try so desperately to hide.' His words echoed in her mind minutes after he had gone, closing the door softly behind him. She could make no sense of them, and it wasn't difficult to dismiss them. She was so uninterested in James and his opinions that an analysis of his cryptic remark would cost more effort than it was worth.

CHAPTER SIX

THE next four weeks brought about a few changes and by the start of June several things had happened. They were not major things, but they made a difference to Deborah's home life and her usual routine.

Her mother had gone back to Amsterdam with Hans Bakker and, after being there for only three days, she had telephoned to say that Hans had proposed and that she had accepted. She was staying on in Holland for a few weeks and would let her family know about the wedding arrangements when she and Hans had made them. This came as a surprise to no one.

James had bought himself a car, a smart white BMW which was brand new and near to the top of the range. It was an expensive car and it seemed somehow to suit James. Deborah had no idea what his financial situation was but she knew he earned good money as a doctor and he probably had some capital behind him. After all, he had worked for years in places where it would have been unnecessary, even difficult, for him to spend his earnings.

He took Sir Henry here and there in the car, the two of them spending a great deal of time together, and this in itself made a difference to Deborah because often her grandfather was not at home when she got back from work. It was either that, or he and James would be at home and there would be visitors in the house, other doctors old and young, and the conversation would be predominantly of a medical nature.

Conversations of this sort were not new to Deborah, of course, and they did not perturb her in the least, even when they took place during meal times, which was mainly when she was sitting in on them. In fact it was interesting to hear James talking about diseases rarely seen in Britain, about pellagra or bilharzia or the various types of malaria he had encountered on his travels. Listening to him brought about in her a respect for him as a doctor, if not as a person, but even so it was a respect she begrudged and would not show ... unlike her grandfather.

Her grandfather. She never had him to herself now, because of James' presence. There were no more one-to-one chats or strolls around the grounds or drives into the country.

So, over the past four weeks Deborah had been going out more often than she used to, alone or with Denis—who was delighted to be seeing more of her. He was surprised, too, that she should be seeking his company about once a week now, and she didn't give him any explanation for the sudden change.

James had asked her out, too. Several times he had asked her to lunch or to join him and Sir Henry when they went out at week-ends. But she declined. Despite her grudging respect for him she still wished him elsewhere and certainly did not want to spend her spare time with him. As it was, she spent more hours than usual in the small sitting room behind the kitchen, a room in which she kept her books and her records, a room which had for years been regarded as Deborah's room, just as the library had always been regarded as Sir Henry's room.

Insidiously, life had changed for her over the past few weeks, just as she had known it would. Thanks to James Beaumont. Still, life was tolerable. It was tolerable, that was, until the day James walked in on her, saying it was high time they had a serious talk.

It was Thursday afternoon, early closing day for her shop, and she was in her sitting room, reading. He didn't knock, he just walked in and settled in the armchair facing her, his long legs stretched out before him. He was wearing a black tee-shirt which clung to the muscles of his broad chest, his big frame filling the armchair as he sat, just looking at her for several seconds before speaking. 'It's time you and I had a talk, Miss Wilson-Courtney.'

She frowned at his tone of voice, at the way he'd addressed her. 'What do you want? I thought you'd gone out with Gramps.'

'I've taken him into town. He wanted to see his solicitor. Max will drive him home later.'

Deborah's frown deepened. 'And what would he want with his solicitor on a Thursday afternoon? Surely Max is working?'

'I've no idea,' James said dismissively. 'I just gave him a lift, that's all. Put your book down, Deborah.'

'Yes, sir.' She slammed her book shut, irked at this invasion of her privacy.

Seeming satisfied, James linked his hands behind his head, smiling slowly, his white teeth making a stark contrast against the darkness of his skin. But there was no humour in his eyes now. 'I'm not going to leave this house, you know. On principle, I won't do that. Not just to please you.'

'I'm aware of that.'

'Good. On the other hand, I hope you realise that I'm not living here in order to punish you.'

'Punish me?' She had no idea what he meant. 'Of course I don't think that.'

'Then why are you behaving the way you are? Why do you vanish every evening after dinner? Why am I constantly getting the cold shoulder treatment?'

Deborah sighed impatiently. 'You're exaggerating. You make me sound completely antisocial. I'm always polite to you, you can't deny that.' She leaned forward, looking directly at him. 'I have no hard feelings towards you, James, but it's true that I'd rather you lived elsewhere. I resent this disruption of my home life in the form of your presence, I resent the way you monopolise my grandfather's time. But I'm aware that he loves you and things will settle down when you take up a new appointment and——'

'And I'm working at the hospital and you see less of me,' he finished, his dark eyes laughing at her.

She nodded. 'Quite.'

James shook his head sadly, looking at her with something approaching distaste. 'I don't like what you're turning into, Deborah, and it's high time I sorted you out before it's too late.'

'Sorted . . .? Too late? You're not making sense.' She spoke with an attitude of boredom. 'And frankly I don't give a damn what you think of me. Besides, you don't know me. You don't know the person I am today.'

'Ah, but I do! I've spent the past four weeks getting to know you. That's surprised you, hasn't it? We've hardly talked, yet I've got to know you far better than you know yourself. And I'm going to tell you about yourself.'

Deborah stared at him, a sudden tug of nervousness contracting her stomach, giving her the urge to get up and walk away from him because she didn't want to hear what he was going to say. She had no idea why she felt like that; there was just something about his tone that alarmed her. 'Look,' she hedged, 'why don't we just call a truce? You get on with your life and I'll get on with mine.'

He ignored that; he carried on with what he wanted to say. 'For the first few days after my return I was amused by your behaviour. Now, I'm sickened by it. I'm also annoyed because your attitude towards me is making your grandfather unhappy, and your "politeness" is fooling no one.

'You made an effort to show me how much you've

changed, but you needn't have bothered. The changes in you are so obvious that I could have seen them with my eyes closed. Once, you were courageous and lively and true to yourself. Oh, it doesn't matter that you made the natural mistakes of a youngster; I'm not talking about your behaviour in those days, I'm talking about your basic personality. *That* has changed. These days you're cowardly and afraid. You're twenty-five years old and you are frightened of men, frightened of living and frightened of yourself. *Wait! . . .*'

As she turned to stare at him, he held up a hand. But Deborah had not been about to speak; his words had robbed her of speech. She thought him crazy! Absolutely mad!

'. . . I've watched you, Deborah. I've listened to you and I've learned about you. Umpteen times you've made remarks like, "Experience has taught me——" or "I've learned from the past that——" And do you know what experience has taught you? Nothing! Do you know how much you've grown during the past few years? Not one little bit!

'You're so busy telling yourself that you've learnt from the past, and you're so busy pointing it out to others that you haven't stopped to realise how you are blocking your own growth as a person and limiting yourself because you're waiting for the past to repeat itself. You haven't learnt from the past, you've been *warped* by it. In fact you're terrified of history repeating itself. You even think this will happen to your mother's marriage. You think she should be "once bitten, twice shy" . . .'

There was no anger in his voice. He spoke with the calm assurance of one who was very familiar with his subject, and his words disturbed Deborah so much that she started instantly to reject them. In her own mind she tried to switch off his voice, to tell herself he was talking nonsense.

'Twice shy. Like you, Deborah? Is this why you go out with Denis Brown, because there's nothing to fear from him? Denis Brown is a camouflage job. I know it, you know it, but I don't expect you'll admit it to me. You think that because you're going out with Denis, you can appear reasonably normal, don't you? If you've got a boyfriend, albeit one who's old enough to be your father, and one you don't see very often, you can pretend that you're not afraid of men.'

That got to her. That was too difficult to reject because it was too near the truth, although she had never thought of herself in terms of actually being afraid of men. She paled considerably but her facial expression did not change. Feeling sick, she kept her eyes on her hands, and she felt sicker as James went on . . . and on.

'You've had several unfortunate experiences with the opposite sex, haven't you? And that's enough for you. At a guess, I'd say it was after Philip whatever his name was that you made up your mind about every other man on earth. You're suspicious of each and every one and you're terrified of any one under forty!'

At that point she tried to speak. She wanted to tell him to go, that she couldn't take any more, but she so desperately wanted to cry that her voice was locked in her throat. Her mouth opened and closed but nothing came out. She would not cry in front of James. She would *not*.

'You're not happy, Deborah. Oh, you're not unhappy, either. You're just—safe. You live in a vacuum, you live by rules and regulations, by a routine which leaves no room for chance, for change, for newness—even for laughter. Four weeks, four weeks I've been here, and not once have I heard you laugh. Do you realise that? Why, you're only half alive!'

He got to his feet, shoving his hands into the pockets of his jeans as he towered over her. 'Just look at you!

Even on your afternoon off you present yourself as the hard-headed business woman that you're not! *False*, everything about you is false. But I know you, I know what's behind this cold veneer, this persona—fear! And it's time you stopped being afraid—of the future as well as the past. You have to stop resenting the past—which includes this childish resentment of *me*. And you'd better get used to a future which includes my presence, because I'm damned if I'll leave this house just to please you and your warped ideas!'

There was a sudden silence, and Deborah's mind spun with all he had said.

'Have you nothing to say, Deborah?' he demanded. 'What is this? Hysterical deafness?'

She glared at him. 'Go to hell.'

'Yes,' he said quietly, unruffled by her reaction. 'The truth can be painful at times. And you've heard the truth today. You can taste it, you can smell it, and you'll do all you can to reject what I've said. But you'll fail. The pretence is over, *Deborah*. Deborah of the cool veneer, Deborah who can't be herself, Deborah who's dishonest and a coward. I much preferred Debbie, with all her faults. At least she didn't deny her own personality, her emotions!'

Something of the girl she used to be surfaced in her at that very moment. She exploded, yelling at him incoherently as she shot to her feet, her arms flying as she tried to hit him, slap him, anything, anything to make him stop talking. This was too painful, too *painful*!

She didn't succeed, of course. He caught hold of her by the wrists, muttering something about her stubbornness and stupidity as he struggled to keep her still. 'Let *go* of me,' she screamed at him. 'I will not allow you to bully me and you'd better learn fast that your strong-arm tactics won't work any more! I'm no longer fifteen years old and you may not——'

Quite what it was that stopped her, she couldn't be sure. So many things happened in such a fleeting time. James' right arm locked firmly around her back as she fought for freedom, holding her so tightly against him that the entire length of her body was touching his, causing her to gasp in shock and distaste.

'Relax!' he ordered, his eyes cold and unreadable. 'You're not too old to be spanked, but I can think of a far better way of bringing you to your senses these days!'

She honestly didn't know what he meant, but she got no further than opening her mouth to protest when suddenly he bent his head and claimed her lips in a kiss which was instantly, disturbingly, intimate.

Deborah went rigid. She couldn't believe what was happening. That the day might come when she would find herself being kissed by James Beaumont had never entered her thinking. With everything in her she tried to pull away from him, hating him in that instant as she had never hated him in the past. Thanks to his hold on her there was no way she could move her body, but she managed to wrench her head away.

Having achieved that much, she could do no more than stare at him, at a loss for words. Overriding her confusion was her awareness of his body against hers, warm and solid. 'What—what was that in aid of?'

'That was an experiment.' The coldness was in his voice now. 'And most unsatisfactory it was. I'll have to try a little harder.'

And with that he kissed her again. This time, she fought harder. The element of surprise was not there the second time and she kept her lips tightly together, struggling against him like a wildcat, not that it did her much good. Her strength was puny against his. His hand came up to hold the back of her head firmly and his mouth parted her lips as he kissed her savagely. She fought him in vain, her mind screaming in protest as his lips ground against hers with a cruelty which did not surprise her. Dear God, he had not changed at all! Time had done nothing whatever to erase the brutal streak in this man, but she would rather have endured his strong-arm tactics of the past than this—this humiliation and degradation!

She was not even aware of it when the turning point came. All she knew was that one moment he was causing her pain both physical and mental, that she was writhing against him and desperately short of breath— and the next moment she was still, actually relaxing against him as his tongue started to probe her mouth and the vice-like grip of his arms slackened to a hold that was comfortable, even comforting.

Then, incredibly, she was kissing him back, encouraging him with her mouth, kissing him with an expertise she didn't know she possessed. As his arms gave her the freedom to move, she instinctively slid her hands around his neck, her fingers curling into the thick blackness of his hair while her body sought to get closer to him.

It was James who called a halt. He put the flat of his hands against her ribs and pushed her gently away from him, and for an instant he looked as disturbed as she felt.

Deborah couldn't think at all. It never occurred to her to speak because she couldn't form a sentence out of the chaos in her mind. She knew only a yearning to kiss him again, to feel the hard strength of his body against hers, the comfort of the strong arms which had during the last few minutes changed from being a prison to a sanctuary... And she was appalled at feeling that way, appalled that she had responded to his kiss. This, after all he had said to her! This, with James, of all the men in the world!

She felt as if she were going mad. She put her hands to her cheeks as she felt the flood of colour rising in them, hating herself for responding to him. And her humiliation was deepened as he spoke, coolly reminding her that his actions had been calculated from start to finish.

'A very worthwhile experiment.' He moved away from her. 'I think that proved much of what I've said to you—that I know you better than you know yourself. You make yourself as unattractive as possible, with that awful hairstyle, with your manner of dressing, with your attitude ... but somewhere inside you there's a real woman waiting to get out.'

'Dear God! I hope you're not thinking that *you're* the man who's going to change me?'

'Would that be so terrible?' He laughed shortly. 'Don't look so horrified, little one. You have nothing to fear from me and there'll be no repeat performance, rest assured.'

'I'm very glad to hear it. So—where do we go from here?'

He shrugged, noting that her tawny eyes were brilliant with anger, uncertainty ... and the threat of tears. 'That's entirely up to you. I've said my piece. We can live as enemies or we can live as friends. Just remember that we'll *both* be living *here*.' He walked to the door, saying she should think things over. 'And perhaps you'll spare a thought for Henry while you're making your decision.'

He closed the door quietly behind him, leaving the room as calmly as he had entered it.

Deborah waited one full minute before going up to her bedroom. Once there, she locked the door and sank into a chair, lacing her fingers together in an effort to stop the trembling of her hands. She felt drained, utterly drained, and within seconds she was crying.

She felt beaten by James in more ways than one. She never had been able to escape him when he decided to tell her a few home truths and today had been no exception. Much of what he said had not been new to her—but some of it was. Never had it occurred to her that she was actually afraid of men. In fact she wasn't. She just didn't want any emotional involvement with them, that's all.

Why not?

The question came as clearly as if James himself had asked it. And the answer . . . it amounted to the same thing. She wanted no emotional involvement because she was afraid of being hurt again. She had loved Philip Forster, she really had loved him . . . although she now had difficulty in recalling the details of his face.

What a fool she had made of herself with Philip! And she was twenty years old at the time. Twenty, for heaven's sake, when she should have been able to trust her judgment.

She had met him on the Fine Arts course she had taken when office work had proved to be the wrong type of job for her, when she had decided to open an antiques shop and had taken the year-long course to learn the trade. Philip had been on the course, too, and they had planned to marry and run a shop together. But how quickly he had disengaged himself when he discovered that she would not inherit her money until she was twenty-five, rather than twenty-one!

And before Philip, briefly, there had been Graham Bennet, who dropped her for someone else. Since Philip, there had been no one, no one until Denis Brown . . .

Yes, Denis was a camouflage job. And yes, she had been deeply affected by the past, far more than she had ever admitted to herself. But James had made her face herself now and she was forced to give thought to the other things he'd told her.

She got up and walked over to the full length mirror in her wardrobe. Did she really make herself as unattractive as possible? Maybe her clothes and her hairstyle were severe but—but nothing. James was right again. Her appearance was designed to minimise any attention the opposite sex might give to her.

But so what? What of it, all of it? People were entitled to change, weren't they? She was the way she was, by choice. And why on earth should she be affected by James' opinions?

She tried to reassert herself, tried not to be affected, but James had certainly given her food for thought, and she resented him for it. She resented the disturbance he had caused in her, about herself. Yet along with that resentment she could not deny that her unwilling respect for him had grown because in so many ways he had been right about her, he had been shrewd enough to see right through her.

Confused again, Deborah lay down on her bed. How could she feel for James two such conflicting emotions, resentment and respect? What sort of—of emotional extortionist was he that he could win from her the latter? And what was she going to *do* about him?

One thing was certain: things absolutely could not go on as they were, not now. Her next encounter with James would be a make or break situation; it would determine what the atmosphere in the house was going to be from now on, and it was already unpleasant enough. What had he said? That they could live as enemies or as friends. He was leaving it to her to decide.

She thumped her pillow. There was, of course, no choice. For her grandfather's sake, she simply had to make an effort. But she would do it *only* for her grandfather's sake!

The housekeeper's tapping on the door broke Deborah's train of thought and she got up reluctantly from the bed.

'What is it, Bessie?'

'Oh! Were you having a sleep? I'm sorry, I didn't realise.' Bessie seemed vaguely surprised, probably because Deborah was not in the habit of taking afternoon naps. 'Sir Henry just phoned. He's going home with his solicitor for dinner. I thought I'd let you know and ask if there's anything in particular you and James might like tonight? I was going to cook the trout for your grandfather but I thought . . . Is anything wrong?'

Deborah was chewing her lip. Nothing and everything was the answer to that question. 'No, not at all. Er— Bessie, I'll discuss dinner with you a little later. I—I want to have a word with James first.'

When the housekeeper retreated, smiling, Deborah went into her bathroom and tidied herself up, satisfying herself that there was no sign of the tears she had shed earlier. Having done that she went in search of James.

He was in the library, reading The Lancet, a medical publication Gramps continued to subscribe to even though he was retired.

James looked at her, his face impassive, his eyebrows raised slightly.

'Gramps is eating with Max and Sophie tonight, and Bessie wondered——' She broke off, smiling a blatantly plastic smile, but it was the best she could manage. She was tense. 'And *I* wondered if you'd like to eat out tonight. I—thought it would be nice to give Bessie a break.'

He didn't make it easy for her. He deliberately misunderstood. 'I don't like eating alone, Deborah, I never did.'

She sighed. 'All right, all right, if you want me to spell it out for you. I'm offering to buy you dinner, James. I'm suggesting that you and I go out to eat together. Now what's your answer? Yes or no?'

'Yes.' There was no hesitation, and he was smiling now. 'Yes, because I like what's on the menu.'

'Eh?'

'An olive branch.' He was still smiling but his dark gaze was taking her apart. 'I am right in thinking that?'

Deborah's answer was not gracious. 'For my grandfather's sake, yes, that's what I'm offering.' She backed out of the room, suggesting they leave the house at eight.

'*Deborah!*'

His tone halted her in her tracks and she fought not to show her annoyance. She failed. 'What now?'

'Your uniform.' He pointed at her. 'If you're going to let your hair down at last, then do it literally. Kindly don't dress like a matron if you're coming out with me. And don't look at me like that! I've told you, you've nothing whatever to fear from me.'

'You really push your luck, don't you?' she said angrily. 'You really push your luck!'

CHAPTER SEVEN

'WHAT the *devil* are you doing?' Deborah spoke to her reflection in the dressing table mirror. It was ten minutes to eight and all the time she had been bathing and getting ready, she had been fuming over James and his orders about how she should dress this evening.

Yet somehow—and it was entirely subconscious—she had ended up complying with those orders even as she'd fumed at his audacity!

She blinked as she realised what she'd done. For the first time in years she had let her hair stay in soft curls around her shoulders. She had also put on her most feminine dress, the sort of thing she would wear for a dinner party or something of that order.

She changed, rapidly, furious with herself for being so affected by James that she had complied with his wishes without realising she was doing so! To hell with that. There were limits! Offering the olive branch was one thing, dressing to please him was quite another!

By eight o'clock she looked as she normally looked: impeccable, smart, her auburn mane secured tightly in a coil with not a hair out of place. And in her opinion she didn't look in the least matronly. *Matronly!* What a cheek he'd had in using that word!

Deborah's surprises were not over. While her afternoon had been disturbing, her evening with James was a strange one. For her, at least, it began strangely and it continued that way.

When she walked into the drawing room and set eyes on him, her breath caught in her throat. He was wearing a suit, a new light grey suit which was beautifully cut and teamed with a crisp white shirt and a silver-grey tie.

He stood as she walked towards him. Her eyes went directly to his and she could hear Joan Clegg's enthusiastic descriptions of him, word for word '... He's got the most attractive suntan, a chiselled and classically handsome face, a superbly muscular physique ... He is gorgeous ... you might have told me how attractive he is!'

How right Joan was! He was all of this, and more, and it was only then that Deborah gave thought to the way he had kissed her that afternoon, to the way she had eventually responded.

'There will be no repeat performance,' he had assured her. 'You have nothing to fear from me.'

She looked at him almost warily now, unsure about—about everything. Unsure that she wouldn't welcome a repeat performance, unsure that she had nothing to fear from him. The crackling vitality she was learning to associate with him filled the room, that nameless aura which kept her eyes riveted on him now.

'Ready?' He said not a word about her appearance, in praise or in criticism, not that she expected any praise.

'I—yes.' For once she was tongue-tied with him, feeling suddenly like a teenager on her first date. 'I—I thought we'd go to——'

'Did you now?' James took her arm and he also took control. 'Well, I've already booked a table for us at Luxton Hall.'

'Luxton Hall?' Deborah's eyes widened in surprise. Luxton Hall had probably the best restaurant in the whole of Yorkshire. It was a stone built, seventeenth century house which was now a hotel, a very expensive hotel with the atmosphere of a comfortable home, and, well, it was hardly the sort of place Deborah had had in mind for this evening ...

James was laughing softly, his brown eyes warm with amusement as he scanned her face. 'Don't look so put out. *I* am taking *you* to dinner. And Luxton Hall is just the right place for a celebration.'

'A celebration? Is this a celebration?'

'I certainly think so.' And with that he offered her his arm.

Deborah was surprised by the gesture, and pleased by it, but as she took his arm and he led her out to his car, she was aware of a tension inside her which she couldn't shake off.

It was still with her when they were halfway to their destination, but James was perfectly at ease, admiring the view and talking about Yorkshire and how much he had missed the Peak District while he had been abroad.

They were driving over Bradfield Moors, towards Wigtwizzle, and being June it was still light enough for them to see the beauty surrounding them. Deborah responded but didn't contribute much to the conversation; she was privately admiring the ease with which James handled the BMW, almost envying his air of relaxation and casualness. This, while at the same time she was wary of the new side of him she was seeing. She was half convinced it wouldn't last, that their evening would end in the inevitable row.

But it didn't. Far from it. From the moment they entered the hotel they were treated with the utmost courtesy and deference, and Deborah felt coddled by the luxury of the place. She also felt coddled by James. He helped her out of the car, held doors open for her, and his hand was at her elbow as they walked. Independent though she might be, these were touches that Deborah appreciated; she was by no means too liberated to enjoy the old-fashioned courtesies from a gentleman.

Heads turned as they walked into the bar for pre-dinner drinks, James drawing several admiring glances from women. The atmosphere was intimate, the lighting subdued, and the room was occupied mainly by couples. Deborah made herself comfortable in a plush chair covered in burgundy-coloured velour, told James what she would like to drink and finally started to relax.

From that moment on she enjoyed herself. Dr James Beaumont was the perfect host, charming, entertaining, attentive and, well, full of surprises because of it!

It wasn't until much later that Deborah realised how skilfully he had drawn her out, encouraged her to talk about herself. But the conversation was kept light throughout the evening, and during a superb dinner (with which they drank champagne) she was constantly amused by James and his tales of the funnier side of living in underdeveloped countries. His experience of the world and its inhabitants was vast, and she was exposed to a dimension of his personality she had never seen before. Maybe it hadn't been there before. Or maybe it had, but she'd been blind to it.

'And you really think you'll settle in Yorkshire now?' She asked the question as they turned into the drive of Vale House, having enjoyed a moonlit ride over hills and dales, taken at an easy pace. The evening was drawing to an end and there followed a moment of potential tension—the only one in hours.

James just looked at her, grinning, but it was enough to make her realise what she'd just asked him. She started laughing, holding her hands up as if in defence as he brought the car to a halt. 'Oh, no! No, honestly, James, there was no hidden meaning in that question!'

His grin changed to a smile, the smile to low laughter which was infectious and almost cheeky. At least, that's how it seemed to Deborah, but she had had far more to drink than she was used to. In fact she rarely drank at all.

'Glad to hear it!' He got out of the car and walked

around the front of it to open the door for her. Deborah watched him by the light of the quaint old lamp which stood at the back of the house, her eyes following his every step.

'And the answer,' he went on, 'is yes. This is what I want now.' He opened his arms in an expansive gesture which embraced everything around them. 'It's settling down time for me ... Looks like Henry's still up.'

Deborah's eyes went momentarily to the house as she stood, her feet crunching against the gravel of the sweeping drive. It was unusual for Gramps to stay up this late; it was past midnight. 'James, I—it's been a lovely evening. Thank you.'

All the amusement left his face and he looked at her for several seconds. 'It's been a wonderful evening, Debbie. Thank you,' he amended, emphasised. 'And it was long overdue.'

She glanced away from him, embarrassed because she could not deny that she had not given James a chance hitherto; her mind had been totally closed to him, she had been stubborn and—and there was something she had to say to him now. She owed him an apology and she must be big enough actually to verbalise it. 'I'm sorry, James.' She held out her hand and he took it, smiling as she shook his hand quite formally. 'You know, I—well, I was so determined to show you that I'm no longer the idiot you used to think me, and yet— yet I ended up behaving like one.'

He held on to her hand as she would have withdrawn it. 'No, don't put yourself down. Don't ever do that.' He let go of her hand and caught hold of her chin, tilting it slightly so he could look straight into her eyes. 'You used to be mixed-up, that's all. You still are, just a little. And you don't really like yourself very much, do you?' He smiled at the surprise on her face. 'Mm. Think about that, because if you don't like yourself, you'll always have trouble in liking other people.'

He did not explain any further. He let go of her chin and walked towards the house, taking hold of her by the arm.

Sir Henry was in his armchair, his nose stuck in a book. 'Well, well, well! This has been quite an evening, one way and another.' His blue eyes took in the pair of newcomers, noting every detail of their appearance, including the flush on Deborah's cheeks.

She went over to him and gave him a hug, planting a kiss on his forehead. 'Hi, Gramps! It's a bit late for you to be up, isn't it?'

One bushy eyebrow rose, drawing laughter from her. 'Buried the hatchet, have you? At last!' It was meant for her ears only and she winked at him.

'James, my boy! I'll have a brandy, if you were about to pour yourself a night cap.'

'I wasn't, but I will.' The younger man laughed. 'So why has this been quite an evening—apart from the shock you had in learning that Debbie and I were out together?'

'Louise phoned. The wedding has been fixed for the last Saturday of this month. All the arrangements have been made.'

'Good!'

'So when are they coming back here?' This, from Deborah.

'They're not. Well, not until after their honeymoon. They're getting married in Amsterdam and there's no reason I can think of that your mother needs to come home first.'

'Oh!' She looked blankly at her grandfather. 'Do you know, I—it just didn't occur to me they'd get married in Holland! I'd taken it for granted they'd get married here.'

'Really?' Gramps shrugged. 'I'd taken it for granted they'd get married there. Still, it doesn't make any difference, except that I won't be going.'

'How come?' James turned to look at him, pausing as he poured the drinks.

'Oh, come on now. I'm too old to go flying off for week-ends abroad.'

'But doesn't Mummy mind?'

'Not a bit. Anyway,' he added mischievously, 'I was at her first wedding. I see no reason I should attend all her weddings!'

'Gramps!' There was laughter all round. Deborah accepted a brandy from James and they all spent half an hour or so discussing the wedding and the arrangements that had been made—down to the last detail.

It was Deborah who went to bed first. 'Well, I'm off. Goodnight, both.'

Sir Henry seemed surprised. 'Running out on us?'

'I have a business to run, and it's Friday tomorrow.'

'And what does that mean?' James asked.

'It means I'm hoping for a busy day.'

'Will you have the energy for a game of squash after work?'

'Squash?' She turned, her hand on the door handle. 'Well, I—yes. But I haven't played for almost a year!'

'Have you got a kit?'

'It's upstairs, gathering dust.'

'Me, too,' he grinned. 'And I haven't played in over a year.'

'Then it sounds like a good idea for both of you,' Sir Henry put in. And that, somehow, settled the matter.

With a wave, Deborah went upstairs, asking James to ring her before leaving the house to pick her up the following evening. She could never be sure what time she finished on a Friday in summer time. If there was business to be done she was not averse to staying open an extra half hour.

She went into her bedroom feeling . . . feeling happy,

young, alive. She acknowledged her feelings with surprise and only then did she pause to think about the hours which had slipped by so rapidly with James. What a day it had been! From the verbal battering he had given her in the afternoon, making it necessary for her to defend herself to herself in the privacy of her bedroom. This, coupled with the realisation that things could not go on as they were between herself and James—to a wonderful evening of laughter and pure enjoyment with him.

Far from sleepy, she got into bed thinking that it had been a strange evening. Strange because it had been shared with him, but she had enjoyed it so! It wouldn't last. She was sure of it. Not that she had any intention of provoking him in any way.

And what of that ... that incident ... during the afternoon? A flash in the pan. It had been a fluke of some kind. After all, she had not been kissed so forcefully by a man in a very long time. She had not been kissed by a man in a very long time.

Explaining it away as a flash in the pan was all very well but—but what about later, when she had walked into the drawing room and felt a tremor of shock on seeing him? That and the inexplicable urge to kiss him there and then, the inexplicable sensation of being drawn to him physically. How could she have felt like that with James? *James!* Hadn't she told her mother, adamantly, that there was no way she could ever think of James as a man, in the context Louise had used the word?

But he was. And she did. Now. Furthermore she would never again be able to think of him in any other context.

It was a very disquieting realisation and Deborah turned off her bedside light with the oddest feeling that James' presence in the house was no longer a nuisance but a ... a potential danger.

She laughed at that idea the next morning. She laughed at Joan, too, when she went into raptures about Holland. Or rather, Deborah's spending a week-end there with James.

'It's only three weeks away,' Joan pointed out unnecessarily. 'And you'll fly out on the Friday afternoon and come back—when? Monday morning?'

'Sunday evening.'

'Why don't you stay on a few extra days and take a look around?'

'What for?'

'To see Amsterdam, of course!' Joan laughed, pushing her specs back into the right position. 'And to have a few days alone with the dishy doctor.' She switched off the kettle and made coffee, something she did every morning just before they opened the shop. 'I tell you, Deborah, I'd do my utmost to wangle that if I were you. I mean, your mother will have left for her honeymoon and you'll have the use of the house—so why not? I can cope on my own here. And now that your relationship with James has taken a turn for the better, you never know . . .' Her voice trailed off as she saw her employer looking at her askance.

'Joan.' Deborah folded her arms across her chest, suppressing a smile at the way the older girl got so easily carried away. 'James and I are just friends. And only just! It might not last, we might be back to square one before we've finished battling it out on the squash courts tonight! In any case I couldn't possibly think of him in a romantic light, so forget that. Honestly, you do get carried away, don't you?'

'I wish I could. Preferably by someone like him.'

Deborah looked heavenward. 'I'll see what I can do. Maybe you'd like to play squash with him tonight? You can take my place.'

'Oh, yes! You can just see me playing squash, can't you, glasses and all!' She grinned impishly, 'Now if it were basketball I might have a chance of impressing the man!' Up came her arm in a gesture of putting a ball into the net. 'I wouldn't even need to jump! No, forget it, Deborah. You might look great in skimpy shorts or a fancy little skirt but the same can't be said for a beanpole like me!' Undaunted, she pursued her earlier theme. 'James will probably be mesmerised by those shapely legs of yours darting around this evening. You'll probably beat him hands down.'

'I intend to try,' Deborah answered seriously. She shook her head, feeling she must make it clear to Joan that she was barking up the wrong tree. 'But James will not be distracted by a pair of shapely legs. Not mine, anyway. He might think of me as a reasonable human being now, but he would never look at me in a sexual light, I'm pleased to say.'

Joan sat down, sipping thoughtfully at her coffee. 'You're not actually related to him, are you?'

The question took Deborah by surprise until she realised what Joan was getting at. 'No, of course not.' She took one look at Joan's face and started chinking with laughter. 'You're incorrigible! There's nothing whatever to prevent my having an affair with him, if that's what you're wondering. Nothing except the fact that we don't fancy each other.' She sobered slightly, wondering if that last remark had been as truthful as it had sounded. 'I've told you, he's not related to us. His mother was a widow, a woman who had worked for years and years as my grandfather's secretary. She died when James was seventeen, a few months before he was to start at the university. Gramps had known James since he was a little boy and because James wanted to be a doctor and because Mrs Beaumont had left no money to speak of, Gramps took the boy under his wing. He brought him to live at Vale House as soon as his mother died, he helped him as much as possible with his studies and everything else and—well, you know the rest.'

Joan nodded, serious now. 'I'd forgotten the details—couldn't remember how the story went.'

The squash game after work was a total disaster for Deborah. It taught her not only that she was out of condition but also how incredibly fit James was. The only sign of the bullet which had been dug out of his thigh was a scar, barely visible beneath the dark hair on his legs. It certainly did not affect his game, neither did his year-long absence from the courts.

When the game was over it was Deborah, breathless and indignant at her appalling score, who suggested they play again the following week. James had wiped the floor with her and was extremely amused by the fact.

'You needn't look so superior,' she called to him as they went their separate ways to the dressing rooms. 'I'm just out of practice, that's all. It'll be different next time.'

She showered and dressed in her one and only pair of slacks and a sweater, and met James as arranged in the café which was part of the sports complex.

'Coffee?' He smiled as she approached the table where he was waiting for her.

'*Two* glasses of orange juice, please. I'm absolutely parched! Shall we have a snack here or can you wait till we get home to Bessie's cooking?'

'I'll get you a sandwich if you like,' he said, standing and glancing at his watch. 'But I've been asked out to dinner at the house of an old friend.'

She didn't bother with a sandwich. She should have realised that James had made arrangements for the evening because he'd phoned during the day to say they should meet at the complex rather than him picking her up from her shop. Joan had been disappointed with the changed arrangement, lamenting that she wouldn't get the chance to say hello to James. He had certainly found a fan in Joan but then he was well liked by everyone—even Deborah was beginning to join those ranks.

She got home by seven forty-five and she was in bed by ten-thirty, her calf muscles letting her know how unfit she was these days.

It wasn't until a few days later that she found out who James had had dinner with, not that she had been particularly curious about it. Over breakfast he reminded her about their next squash game.

'Your granddaughter didn't put up much of a match for me last week,' he informed Gramps, who was in the corner of the conservatory scrutinising his fish. He was so intent upon their movements that he didn't hear, and James smiled, turning to Deborah. 'I think he's been hypnotised. So what about tonight, after work?'

'Oh, I can't!' She was genuinely sorry. 'I've got a date with Denis. He's taking me to the City Varieties Music Hall in Leeds. He booked some time ago.'

Sir Henry tuned in to that. He let out a bark of laughter and turned to look at her, grinning from ear to ear. 'Isn't that the place where everyone dresses in Edwardian clothes? Audience and all?'

'It doesn't sound like your scene.' James was having difficulty suppressing a smile. 'An old time music hall and Edwardian clothes? Is this what happens when you go out with middle-aged men?'

'Don't get carried away, James. The audience only dress up like that when the television cameras are there. But they're not at the moment—and Denis and I are seeing a regular show. And don't,' she added, laughing, 'be cheeky about Denis.' Of course he'd only been teasing, she knew, and she took it in the spirit in which it was meant. 'Shall we play squash tomorrow, then?'

Gramps answered for him, taking his seat at the breakfast table as Bessie came in. 'James is going to a party tomorrow night.'

'Anyone I know?' Deborah asked.

'The party-giver or my escort?'

'Either.'

'You don't know the party-giver. He's fairly new to the area, a consultant at the Jessop Hospital for Women—obstetrics and gynaecology. That's where Diane works, too. She's a Theatre Sister.'

'Diane?'

'The lady I'm going to the party with. Diane Massey. Don't you remember her? She's an old friend, the one I had dinner with last week. I brought her home once or twice in the past.'

'Can't say that I do.' Deborah found herself trying hard to remember, and her memory was a long one. She had probably not met the girl. It was on the tip of her tongue to ask what Diane looked like, how old she was and so on. She could have, James wouldn't have minded in the least, but because she caught herself feeling a little too curious about the girl, she ended up saying nothing.

It was Gramps who brought them back to their original subject. 'What's wrong with Thursday? You could play in the afternoon, it's your half day, Debbie.'

She clicked her tongue, looking apologetically at James. 'I'm going to an auction in Leicester on Thursday. It's at an old rectory and they're selling——'

'Really?' James' interest was caught. 'May I come with you? I'd be very interested to watch and——'

'Of course! I'd like that. It'll mean we can share the driving.'

James looked heavenward and then at Gramps. 'Charming, that! Eh, Henry?'

The old man's eyes were twinkling. 'As you say, lad. Still, you know what to do to teach her a lesson for her tactlessness.'

'Yes. And I will.'

And he did.

Deborah did all the driving on Thursday, there and back. James bought her a splendid lunch, however, and it was during this that they talked on a serious level for the first time. They talked history, they talked politics and music. By the end of the day they had discussed poetry and literature, too, and she was surprised and pleased to discover how frequently her views and likes tallied with his. Not for one moment had she thought he would know anything about poetry, but she was wrong.

They ended the day in her sitting room where Deborah kept most of her books, browsing and nattering, Sir Henry having gone to bed some time earlier. It was almost one in the morning when Deborah made a move, saying she would leave James with her books and see him at breakfast.

'I'm honoured,' he glanced meaningfully around the room which was regarded as being her private space.

'You are,' she agreed. 'But I think you're worthy. Just about.'

'Thanks,' he grinned, settling back again in the armchair. 'Goodnight, Debbie.'

'Goodnight.' She'd taken two strides along the hall when she remembered something she'd meant to ask him. She opened the sitting room door just as James had got up to go after her and they collided with each other very inelegantly.

'Hell, I'm sorry!'

'I'm so sorry!'

James' hands went immediately to her arms to steady her, laughing apologetically because he'd almost knocked her over. She was instantly aware of and disconcerted by his touch, managing with difficulty to join in his laughter. She could feel colour rising in her cheeks and she cursed herself for it because his hold tightened on her and his eyes immediately probed hers. 'Are you all right?'

'Of course.' But her voice came out too quietly because his touch was making her tingle with pleasure. There was a moment, just a few seconds of silence, of stillness, as her tawny eyes met with his. She wanted him to kiss her, was even willing him to.

But already he had let go of her and her blush deepened at the thoughts she'd had.

'You wanted to say something?' His eyebrows rose slightly, probably at the stupid blush on her cheeks and she looked away from him.

'I—I can't remember what it was.' Nor could she. 'It'll come to me at breakfast. I—must go,' she went on, a little too quickly, making matters worse even as she strove for lightness. 'Must get my quota of beauty sleep.' She took a step sideways, uncomfortable with his proximity.

'In that case you could afford to stay up half the night with me, at least.'

The deep voice was quiet, serious, and she turned to look up at him as she'd started to leave the room, wanting to see whether there was amusement in the dark brown eyes.

There wasn't. But the moment was over because James went back to his chair, bidding her goodnight for the second time, both of them forgetting he'd wanted to say something to her.

Deborah put her hands to her cheeks when she got into her bedroom, angry with herself for blushing so easily in front of him. Heavens, what was wrong with her? She was not normally in the habit of blushing—over anything! Nor was she in the habit of wanting to be kissed. Far, far from it. But just now there had been a moment when——

'What the devil's got into you?' She was talking to her reflection again. She seemed to be doing a lot of that lately. 'You're out of order. You're looking for trouble carrying on like that, even if it is only in your head.'

That's where it would stay, too. Even if she were interested in James as more than a friend, that interest would not be reciprocated. To him she was just Debbie. Little Debbie.

She pulled the pins from her hair rather cruelly, wincing as she tugged at the elastic band. When she had stripped off her jacket and blouse she caught sight of herself again. Her hair was tumbling all over the place, her firm breasts provocative in the lacy bra. Would he be more inclined to kiss her if he saw her looking like this? No. He'd seen her looking like this.

'You're being ridiculous,' she told herself firmly. And how he would laugh if he knew what had gone through her mind! She must keep her emotions out of her friendship with James. All of them. Hadn't experience taught her——

That thought was cut off by the memory of his words. 'You haven't learned from the past, you've been warped by it!' *Warped* by it. Had she? Maybe. He had surely put it too strongly but even so, even if the woman in her were to make a comeback, it should not be for James' benefit. He wouldn't appreciate it, anyway.

The woman in her? What was she thinking! She never had been a *woman*. She had been a girl, a girl with too many dreams and ideals. In those days she had wanted marriage and children, lots of them. But that was not, definitely not, what she wanted for herself now. Life was good as it was. Very good.

During the next three weeks life got even better. She spent much of her spare time with James, playing squash games she never won, tennis likewise, swimming, riding, driving, walking and occasionally going to the theatre. She had seen most of the current theatrical productions with Denis but she saw two of them for a second time with James. She continued to see Denis every week because she could think of no reason not to, and James went out as frequently with Diane Massey. During the week-ends, Gramps joined them when they drove into the country. They visited Chatsworth House, not for the first time, of course, and spent a pleasant day in Matlock. For Gramps' benefit they went to the botanical gardens in Sheffield where they saw the aviary and, more interesting to Gramps, the aquarium.

Mainly she and James were alone, though, because Sir Henry had the benefit of James' company during the day when Deborah was working. There were two more occasions when they had casual physical contact, once in the confines of the car and once on the tennis courts, when Deborah had had the feeling that he would take her in his arms as he had once before. But James had meant it when he'd said there would be no repeat performance and there were moments when he seemed deliberately to move away from her, almost as if her closeness were distasteful to him.

That bothered her enormously. Distasteful, she knew, was far too strong a word. Undesirable was nearer the mark, yet equally thought-provoking. And she did think about it. Why? Why did he seem to avoid her, why did he avoid all physical contact?

The female in her, or perhaps it was purely her ego or vanity, responded to this, to the challenge it presented. She was moving slowly towards the point of frustration, the point where she made up her mind to change things. Just once. She was an attractive girl; he had said as much to her more than once, in the present and in the past. Just once she wanted him to acknowledge her as something other than Little Debbie. Having achieved that, she would be content to revert to the status quo. After all, life was good at the moment and her friendship with James had become very valuable to her.

On the evening before they flew to Holland she and James went out to dinner, alone. They left Sir Henry perfectly content with the visitors who had descended on him.

For the occasion Deborah let her hair down both literally and figuratively. She did not go overboard in her choice of dress, not wishing to be obvious in any way. She wore a simple pale blue shift in a soft, clingy material, about which he made no comment, though he did make a casually approving remark about her hair. She even went as far as flirting with him in the subtlest way. But at the end of the evening, when she was thanking him warmly for a lovely time, he just tapped her lightly on the nose with his forefinger, smiled and said he'd enjoyed it, too.

Deborah went to her bedroom fuming, fuming over something she would never be able to complain about to him! The wretched man.

CHAPTER EIGHT

LOUISE was chatting incessantly as they all drove from the airport to Hans' house, pointing out this and that to James and Deborah. Hans was at the wheel, laughing from time to time and remarking how his future wife had fallen in love with Amsterdam and how she had already seen almost everything there was to see.

'I can understand that,' Deborah said enthusiastically. It was still light and she was enjoying her first impressions of the city from the car windows.

'A city of bicycles,' James remarked.

'Very much so. And bridges and flowers and—there are more than one thousand bridges, did you know that?' The question came from Hans but he didn't give anyone a chance to answer. 'From the simplest brick structures to huge drawbridges. Of course we're not short on canals, either!' he went on drily, provoking laughter all around.

His house overlooked just one of myriad canals, the Prinsengracht, and stood in the old part of the city. It was a seventeenth century structure, very tall, very narrow but very deep, an oddly shaped house on the front of which was a charming, bell-shaped gable. Just as Deborah was thinking it far too big for one couple, her mother explained that the two top floors of the house were let to a family; they had a separate entrance and they all lived quite privately under one roof.

This still left more than enough space for Louise and Hans, and Deborah was enchanted with the place as she and James were shown the various rooms. It had an air of cosiness and subdued colour and it gave one the feeling that time had stood still for many years in this building.

'Lovely, isn't it?' Louise looked expectantly at her daughter.

'Charming, absolutely charming!' Deborah gave her a brief hug, noting with pleasure the glow on her mother's cheeks, the light in her eyes. 'I'm sure you'll be very happy here ... Oh, that reminds me, I have something for you!'

They settled in the sitting room, drinking freshly ground coffee, and Deborah handed over the wedding gifts she and James had bought together with the envelope Sir Henry had sent.

Louise opened it and sat quietly for a moment reading the letter from her father with which there was a small, folded piece of paper, a cheque which was their wedding present. She looked up with tears in her eyes and silently handed the envelope and its contents to Hans.

'How very, very generous!' Hans was equally touched. 'I must phone him at once.' He got up to do just that and Louise went with him to the hall, where the telephone was.

James and Deborah exchanged smiles.

Nine o'clock saw the arrival of three more people, relatives of Hans who had driven some distance to attend the wedding and who would be staying the night. At nine thirty the whole party went out to dinner and by the time they got home, a little before midnight, Louise was showing signs of wedding nerves.

She needn't have worried. The civil ceremony the following afternoon lasted only half an hour or so and it went very smoothly indeed. By three o'clock the entire party was back at the house, being twenty-seven people in all, just relatives and close friends, and the hubbub of chatter, congratulations and speeches began. Caterers had been brought in for the occasion and did a splendid job, clearing everything away quietly and unobtrusively as time went on and leaving the house as pristine as they had found it.

Louise's planning had been impeccable. She and her new husband were due to leave Holland in the early evening, for a month-long honeymoon in Germany, Belgium and France, at the end of which they would come to England so that Louise could arrange the shipment of her belongings from Vale House.

An elderly man, a retired university lecturer and Hans' oldest friend was, with his wife, to drive the newlyweds to the airport. James and Deborah did not go with them because they'd been invited to have dinner with one of the wedding guests whose home was a houseboat on the canal outside!

It was during the goodbyes and well wishing that Louise mentioned the idea of having a birthday party for her father. 'Darling,' she put a small, beautifully wrapped package into her daughter's hands. 'It's your birthday next week, and I'll be away, so take this now but don't open it before the thirtieth of June!'

'I won't.' Deborah laughed.

'And I've been thinking——'

'Louise, we really must go.' Hans was getting twitchy about leaving for the airport.

'One minute, darling.' She turned back to her daughter. 'Daddy's going to be seventy-five in the first week of August. Hans and I will be at Vale House by then and I think it would be nice to have a party for him, don't you? Seventy-five is——'

'It's a lovely idea!' Both Deborah and James were very much in favour. 'We'll invite everyone, all his friends and——'

'I must go now,' Louise cut her off apologetically. 'You'll have to make the arrangements. Perhaps you and Bessie can put your heads together and sort it out?'

'Of course See you in a month. Best of luck!'

'Happy honeymoon!' James kissed Louise and shook hands with Hans.

'Thank you.' Hans was grinning. 'Here, James, my car keys. You know where it is. Use it by all means. You might decide to stay on for a couple of days and take a look at our interesting city. You've got the house keys, there's stacks of food in the frezer and—dear me, we *must* go!'

Half an hour later, when she and James were finally alone in the house, Deborah looked thoughtfully at the clothes she had brought with her. She had brought more than she needed for a week-end, so she wasn't stuck for something to wear but what would be appropriate for dinner on a houseboat moored on a canal? And their hostess was a sixty year old lady who painted for a living and wore clothes which were, well, unusual to say the least! Unconventional, was the way Louise had described this lady with whom she had become friends. Of course they had their painting in common but Deborah couldn't see that they had anything else in common. Brigitte Hinze was forceful, forthright and . . . perhaps just a little weird. It was sweet of her, though, to ask them to dinner.

Deborah decided to confer with James. She tapped on the door of the guest room across the hallway from her own room. There was a vanity unit and washbasin in this room and that was where James stood, shaving with an electric razor.

He was naked but for a towel around his waist and her eyes went instantly to the broad expanse of his back, watching the play of muscles in the seconds before he turned to face her.

'What was that?' He switched off his razor.

Her eyes moved fleetingly over the broad and muscular chest covered with a mass of dark hair. She glanced away briefly before looking directly at him. 'I— hadn't spoken. But I was going to ask you how you're going to dress tonight.'

His eyebrows went up. 'I thought I'd wear clothes.'

She giggled. 'Come on, I didn't think you'd go in a bath towel! I mean, are you wearing a suit or——'

'Not likely! No suit, no tie, just slacks and a shirt. I suggest you do likewise—according to Hans, Brigitte does not live alone. She has *seven* cats and, it seems, we're honoured to be asked to her place. He says she lives like a hermit for most of the time but just occasionally she goes mad and throws a dinner party.'

'Well, she certainly took a shine to you this afternoon.'

'Really? I thought she took a shine to you.'

They laughed. Deborah backed out of the room as he switched his razor on. 'Okay. See you in ten minutes or so.'

She didn't have a pair of slacks with her and any that she found in her mother's wardrobe wouldn't fit. Stumped because her own clothes were all smart and expensive, she put on a black and white dress with a matching jacket (a simple outfit in material which made her think of a chess-board) and shrugged philosophically.

Their evening was riotous, not at all what they'd expected. Apart from the cats, Brigitte was surrounded by a dozen or more people whom, she said, she had decided only an hour ago to invite round for drinks.

There was no dinner, as such. There were dips and crisps and nuts and sandwiches. One young man, long-haired and young enough to be his hostess's grandson, spent most of the evening in the kitchen cooking delicious feather-light pancakes which were snatched up as soon as they left the pan. He told Deborah goodnaturedly that this was why he had been invited—to produce *pannekoeken*!

Everybody spoke English, most extremely well, and Deborah and James were constantly entertained, amused and questioned about themselves and the sort of lives they lived in the north of England. Deborah had already warmed to the Dutch and she enjoyed herself enormously. Everybody offered to show her and James the sights, everybody insisted they should stay on in the city and by the end of the evening she was very much in favour of the idea, though she wouldn't commit herself without asking James what he thought.

By the end of the evening she was also tipsy, having drunk several tots of genever—Dutch gin that is sipped without ice or a mixer (or so Brigitte insisted) in small glasses. Deborah hadn't liked it at first, but it had started to grow on her and, somehow, her glass seemed to have been replenished every time she picked it up. But by the time she and James had walked slowly back to their temporary home, the night air had helped a little and she was thinking clearly enough to discuss the idea of their staying on.

By unspoken agreement they headed straight for the kitchen and a cup of tea. 'What do you think?' Deborah was searching in cupboards for biscuits and cakes and she turned to look at James when an answer was not forthcoming.

'If you'd like to, we could stay a few days,' he said at length, and a little reluctantly. 'But what about your shop?'

'Joan can cope perfectly well.' She did not add that she'd already been assured by Joan on this point! 'All I'd have to do is ring her and let her know.'

'I must say I'd rather we went exploring on our own. Going around with those people we met tonight doesn't appeal to me. They were friendly enough but——'

'But a bit much,' Deborah interrupted. 'I agree entirely.' She'd found the biscuit tin and was putting some on a plate.

James said nothing. He seemed intent on the cup of tea in front of him.

'You seem reluctant, James. You haven't got any

commitments at home, have you? An interview or
something?'

'Not yet. Not until mid-July.'

When this was followed by another silence from him
she said, 'Okay. You're obviously not keen so let's
forget the idea. We'll go home tomorrow as planned.'
She put the plate of biscuits on the table, a little
disappointed and vaguely irritated with him.

He looked up quickly. 'Hey, hey, there's no need to
slam the crockery around! I've already said we'll stay
on if you'd like to.'

'Do me no favours.'

His hand snaked out to encircle her wrist. 'Don't get
stroppy with me, little one. I'm only thinking——'

She wouldn't have, if he hadn't called her that, if it
hadn't been for the warning note in his voice. 'I've told
you, forget it! The subject's closed.'

He got leisurely to his feet, his hand tightening on her
wrist as he did so. Quietly, slowly, he said, 'Discovering
Amsterdam with you, bright eyes, is a very appealing
idea. But I'm not sure that it's a good idea for us to be
alone in this house for a week or so. That's the only
reason I hesitate.'

Her irritation vanished and she started laughing,
eyes bright with amusement now as she looked up at
him. 'What are you talking about? It's no secret to
anyone that we live together in England!'

'With Henry and Bessie,' he added pointedly, letting
go of her wrist. He wasn't at all amused, he was treating
the issue seriously. 'But if you're happy with the
arrangement, then so am I.'

'You don't sound very happy.' She took a small step
forward placing herself unnecessarily close to him, her
attitude, her eyes, challenging him. 'You're sure you
don't feel . . . threatened, perhaps?'

'Threatened? You're the one who might feel
threatened.'

She laughed softly, reaching out to tug gently at his shirt as she mocked him with her eyes. 'I don't feel threatened, James, but perhaps you do?' And with that she moved fractionally, provocatively closer.

It worked. She got the response she wanted ... but she also got more than she bargained for. His eyes moved fleetingly to her lips and then he was kissing her, his arms closing around her waist.

With a feeling of triumph Deborah parted her lips against the gentle pressure of his mouth. She moved her body very subtly against his, determined that he would acknowledge her fully as a desirable woman.

But it all went wrong.

The kiss deepened and he explored her mouth intimately, erotically, and she responded far more than she had planned on, kissing him hungrily as a liquid heat started to spread through her body. In the recesses of her mind she knew a vague feeling of alarm even as her pulses leapt and accelerated dizzyingly. She wanted more than an acknowledgement from him, she *wanted* him!

She pulled away, alarm turning to fear. This wasn't supposed to happen! All she had planned on was ... James' hold was too firm to allow her escape. His arms moved down to her hips and tightened. He shifted his stance slightly, pulling her between the hardness of his thighs as his mouth once again sought hers.

She struggled against him and he let go of her at once, his hands taking her firmly by the shoulders as he held her at arms' length.

'Games, Debbie?' At least he wasn't amused by her panic. His eyes were almost black as they scanned her face, and she could well imagine what she looked like to him, flushed, startled, nonplussed. 'No,' he said quietly, 'I don't feel threatened. But are you *quite* sure that you don't?'

'I——' She shrugged his hands away and sank on to a

chair with as much nonchalance as she could muster. She was trembling inside. 'Of course not. You've—told me I have nothing to fear from you.'

'You haven't . . . though I wouldn't advise you to test me too often. Assuming that was some sort of test?'

'It was neither a test nor a game, James. It just—it just happened.'

'I see.' He sat down and picked up his tea.

She glanced at him quickly, wondering what he was really thinking. She had instigated what had just happened; she had provoked him, and she felt no sense of triumph now. By reminding him that he'd told her she had nothing to fear from him, she had given herself away. In as many words she had admitted she was afraid . . . of intimacy, of emotional involvement.

James knew that already, of course. It was only her admission of it that was new to him. New to her was the realisation that he'd been right when he told her she was a little mixed up. She was. More so now than when he'd said it.

She glanced at him again and again as she sipped at her tea. Only now was she beginning to realise how much depth there was to this man. He really did know her very, very well. He was also sensitive to her feelings, and that was something she had never given him credit for. Didn't he have the perfect opportunity, right now, to tease her mercilessly about the way she had panicked in his arms? But he wasn't saying a thing, and he knew full well she'd lied when she'd said it 'just happened'.

She groaned inwardly, feeling incredibly foolish now. God, how transparent she must be to him! 'James, I——'

'Leave it,' he said quietly. 'There's no need for a post-mortem or explanations of any kind. There's one thing you need to be told, however, though it's something you ought to be aware of already. You are beautiful, intelligent and desirable. Very desirable.'

'Why . . .' Confused, she stared at him. 'Why are you saying that?'

'Because it's true. Because you need to have it confirmed, since you're so lacking in confidence. What happened just now is no big deal but be careful, please, because I don't want our friendship to get—complicated. On the other hand, I'm not made of stone . . .' He left the warning hanging in the air and got to his feet. 'I'll check the doors now and then I'm off to bed. We'll plan our sight-seeing in the morning, eh? Goodnight, Debbie.' He closed the kitchen door behind him.

Deborah put her elbows on the table and stuck her head in her hands. Good grief, how much he had managed to say in so few words! And how rapidly was her confusion clearing!

He did not want their friendship to get complicated. He'd given her the confirmation of her attractiveness she needed, but he didn't want her . . . while on the other hand he would not be responsible for the consequences if she made another pass at him. After all, she was desirable. In other words, *she* should keep her distance!

He'd said all of this but he had not put her down or embarrassed her. He'd been—clinical, like the doctor that he was. Suddenly she was laughing, her respect for him soaring even though she couldn't decide whether she had been praised by him or told off! 'What a curious man you are!' she muttered. 'I wish I understood you as well as you understand me.'

But she was a babe in comparison to him, intellectually and in every other respect!

Bemused, she went to her room and thought about him for almost two hours before she went to sleep. No wonder she dreamed about him.

The following week was marvellous, full of surprises

and laughter and discovery. Deborah cooked breakfast every morning and they ate out every evening, always at a different place. They frequented restaurants and the so-called 'brown cafés', the haunts to which Amsterdammers retreated, usually after dinner in their own homes. These places varied in comfort and decor if not so much in ambience and the sociability of their customers, not that foreigners were encouraged into them. Brown cafés being neighbourhood gathering places, not tourist traps. But Deborah and James wanted to see some local colour and in these establishments everybody talked to everybody. They didn't mind sitting in old taverns where the surroundings were heading towards dilapidation—or standing, for that matter, when there weren't enough seats.

By contrast they had dinner and spent a pleasant evening in the luxury of a hotel when it was Deborah's birthday—a surprise James sprang on her, as was the cashmere sweater he presented her with.

She had had to buy a few clothes, jeans and blouses, because after two days of using Hans' car they abandoned it and hired bicycles instead. It was by this method of transport that they explored the great city squares, the Frederiksplein, the Rembrandtsplein, the Thorbecksplein, the last of which being a down-market section full of girlie bars ... but interesting to see nonetheless.

More sobering was their visit to the Municipal Theatre, the Van Gogh museum, the Rijksmuseum and several others. They didn't see all there was to see, of course; to achieve that would have necessitated their staying longer than a week and, much as she would have liked to, Deborah had to think of Joan coping by herself at the shop. June had slipped into July and that was one of the busiest months for people visiting the Peak District.

They spent their last afternoon in Vondel Park,

sitting on a bench and eating the lunch they had bought. They had bought their lunch on most days at *broodjes-winkels*—Dutch sandwich shops which sold a myriad of cheeses and cold cuts served in fresh buns.

'Come on, James.' Deborah shook the crumbs from her clothes and got to her feet. 'We have a bit of shopping to do before we call it a day.'

He grimaced at the word. 'Shopping? Sounds ominous. You're not going hunting for presents, are you?'

'Just a few,' she said innocently. 'And I want a pair of those *klompen* as a souvenir.'

'What?'

'You know, those painted clogs we saw in that shop. I fancy a pair.'

'Oh, Debbie! What a typical tourist you're turning out to be! I'm disappointed in you——'

'Come on, this won't take long.'

'And when are you going to wear painted wooden clogs, might I ask? Or are you going to hang them on your bedroom wall?'

She struck her nose in the air and ignored him.

'All right, all right, I'm coming.'

It was seven o'clock when they got back to the house and they flopped into chairs, shattered. James wagged a finger at her. 'You conned me, madam! That was the longest afternoon I've spent in years and as a punishment *you* can cook the dinner tonight.'

They had decided to eat at home tonight and to go to bed at a reasonable hour because they had to get up early to leave for the airport next day. And James had said he would cook dinner, since she had made breakfast for him daily. 'But you said——'

'And you said it would be a swift shopping trip. You've bought presents for everyone from the gardener to the milkman.'

She burst out laughing, tossing back her mass of very windblown hair. 'Don't exaggerate so!'

'In the kitchen,' he said firmly, jerking a thumb towards the door. 'Now. I'm starving.'

She cocked her head to one side, looking at him very impishly. 'Couldn't I take a bath first?'

'Now! Or I'll put you over my knee!'

She scampered. She went to the kitchen and he went to the bathroom. Ah, well ... he'd just have to put up with a scruffy-looking female at the dining table tonight. She was wearing jeans and a grubby blouse and she looked as though she'd been cycling through the heart of Amsterdam in the rush hour.

'My God, you look a mess!' James made the pronouncement when they were half way through dinner. 'But the food is marvellous!'

She just looked at him. How did one answer two such diverse remarks?

He stretched out on the settee when dinner was over, in a very good humour now he'd been fed. 'You may now have your bath,' he told her as she drained her coffee cup. 'I shall wash up.'

'How kind!' She curled up in the chair and put her head back. The next thing she knew, she was asleep. She opened her eyes half an hour later to find James watching her.

'Was I dozing?'

'No, you were sound asleep. Looking like an angel. How deceiving appearances can be.'

She made a face at him and got to her feet, stretching. 'Put some fresh coffee on, would you, James? I'll be down by the time it's ready.'

She had a hot bath, washed her hair, dried it and stepped into a clean pair of jeans and a tee-shirt. The clogs were on her bed and she put them on, giggling at the sight of them. In bright red they were gaudy, to say the least, but fun, and not uncomfortable. She had bought a leather belt for James when he strayed from her side for a few minutes in one of the shops they'd been in. She took it from her bag now; it wasn't gift-wrapped but there was nothing she could do about that.

'Coffee's ready!' His voice came booming up the stairs to her.

'On my way.'

She almost made it, too. She had only four more stairs to descend when suddenly she found herself in a crumpled heap on the floor of the hall.

Dazed more than hurt, or so she thought, a loud cry escaped from her as she scrambled to her feet—which were now minus the clogs. One of them was on the bottom stair and the other was two yards along the hall, as was the paper bag she'd been carrying.

She was falling again when James' arms closed around her. 'What the devil——?'

'My ankle!' She yelped as she put her foot down, leaning heavily against him. Tears sprang to her eyes and she knew only gratitude as he lifted her into his arms.

He put her gently on the settee, calm, cool, but not very pleased with her. 'Those blasted clogs ...' He looked up to see the tears on her cheeks and he shook his head slightly, putting a hand to her face to brush them away with his thumb. 'It's all right, Debbie. Now, let's take a look at you.' His voice turned professional.

Automatically the doctor in him took over and he eased her against the cushions, in a sitting position. He lifted her hand, which she was rubbing frantically at her knee, then he reached for the waistband of her jeans. 'Easy now. Let's get these off. Put your weight on your hands and——'

'I'm all right!' she protested. Stupidly. 'I—it's just my ankle, there's no need to—to fuss.' She finished the sentence lamely. What she meant was that she didn't want to take her jeans off—and she knew that he knew it. She knew also how pathetic he would think her.

He just looked at her. He just looked at her and waited until she did what he'd told her.

Blushing furiously at her own stupidity she unzipped her jeans, put her weight on her arms and allowed him to ease the jeans from her so that she was caused the minimum of discomfort.

Blood was trickling from a small cut on her knee but there was no swelling or discolouration around it.

'All right, your knee and your ankle. Anything else? Did you hurt yourself anywhere else?'

'No,' she said dully. 'And the knee's okay but my ankle is throbbing like mad. It's probably sprained.'

James, of course, was the judge of that. He examined her ankle and moved his fingers expertly over her feet and her legs, probing gently around the cut knee. Only then did he allow himself to smile. 'Your diagnosis is correct.'

'Of course it is!' She spoke with brave indignation. 'I've lived with a consultant orthopaedic surgeon for the past ten years, I must have learned something! A sprain is the wrenching of ligaments at a joint. If there's been a blow it might be accompanied by a fracture—which it isn't.' She laughed as his eyebrows went up. 'Impressed?'

'Not in the least. Treatment?'

'Cold compresses. The first aid box is——' But James had already left the room, laughing.

He came back with the first aid box which lived in full view on top of the bathroom cabinet, attended to her knee and spent half an hour applying cold compresses to her ankle in the hope of reducing the swelling. With deft fingers he then supported the joint with thick padding of cotton wool interleaved in firm turns of a bandage.

With a towelling dressing gown draped around her, which she enjoyed because it was his, she was then given the coffee she'd been coming down for when she took the tumble. 'James ... thanks. It's feeling tons better already, thanks to your quick action.'

'We'll see how it is in the morning. We can always go home a few days later if——'

'No, no! I'll be fine, really. It's not too bad, and I can't leave Joan——'

'I said we'll see.' Which put an end to the discussion.

She could have walked up the stairs, actually, when they went to bed later on. With a little help, that is.

'No, James, I don't want you to carry me. There's no need! With the banister on one side and you on the other I'll——'

'Have you got masochistic tendencies I know nothing about?' he admonished, scooping her up before she could do anything to stop him. 'Why give yourself unnecessary discomfort?' He carried her to her bedroom as though she weighed nothing more than a bouquet of flowers. 'I'll help you with——'

'No. *No.*' She absolutely was not going to let him help her take off the rest of her clothes!

'Debbie, for heaven's sake. I'm——'

'A doctor, and you've seen it all before. I know, I know. To hell with that.' She shrugged the dressing gown from her shoulders and handed it to him, ignoring the amusement in his eyes. 'If you'll just give me my nightie, it's in the wardrobe there ...'

'Pretty.' He handed her the pale lemon nightie.

'Thank you. Goodnight, James.'

'Listen, if you can't sleep, give me a shout. I'll give you the pain killers I offered you earlier. You know, I've never looked after anyone as disobedient as you. It's all well and good not liking to take tablets but——'

'Yes, doctor.'

'Wretched girl!'

'Yes, doctor.'

'It's no good smiling at me like that, you stubborn wench!' But he bent down, nevertheless, to kiss her forehead.

'Do you kiss all your patients goodnight?'

'Only the pretty ones.' And then he was gone.

Deborah switched off the bedside lamp. Her ankle was throbbing a little but it wasn't going to stop her sleeping.

An hour later she was still awake. But it had nothing to do with her ankle. She was thinking about James and she couldn't rid him from her mind. She was reliving the week they had spent together, the laughter, the jokes, the teasing, the sights they'd seen.

Inexplicably her eyes suddenly filled with tears and she felt strangely depressed. The hands on the bedside clock moved steadily on and she couldn't seem to shake the sadness which had washed over her.

'James?' He was moving about. She heard his bedroom door open, the creak of the floorboards on the landing.

A crack of light seeped under her bedroom door and she switched on the bedside lamp as he answered her summons. 'Can't sleep?'

She fiddled with the bedclothes so she wouldn't have to look at him while she lied. 'Oh, I've been sleeping but I've just woken up and I'm parched.' She glanced at him as she said the last couple of words and he nodded, raking his thick, black hair back with lean fingers.

He disappeared for a few moments and came back with a glass of water and two tablets which he dropped into her hand, the expression on his face telling her he would brook no argument this time. She took them and he sat on the edge of her bed while she did so. He took the glass from her, put it on the bedside table and . . . and Deborah didn't know what came over her just then.

She felt the sting of tears at the back of her eyes, heard the soft moan she emitted as she leaned her head against his shoulder. She sighed as his arms came comfortingly around her and she spoke without thinking what she was saying. 'I love you, James . . .'

He moved her gently away from him, his hands on her arms, looking at her with not the slightest trace of surprise, but looking at her hard ... 'I'm glad to hear it. I'm fond of you, too, little one.' He was smiling now and his hand went to her forehead.

Debroah's eyes widened. He was patronising her! He seemed to think she was rambling or something! 'I mean it, James.'

Very fleetingly there was a play of emotions on his face which she couldn't interpret. There was a slight smile, a frown, something resembling bewilderment in his eyes and then, 'You're tired, Debbie. If we are leaving tomorrow you'd better get some more sleep. It's three in the morning and I think we could both do with that, mm?'

She lowered her eyes as his hands closed over hers and gave them a reassuring squeeze. He was right not to believe her. She didn't know what had made her talk like that. He was right in saying she was tired. And she was probably feeling a little vulnerable after her accident this evening. Probably it was gratitude that she was really feeling toward him. He had been very kind to her, after all.

She was still mulling it over as she drifted to sleep, writing off what she had said as meaningless, untrue. Perhaps her physical attraction towards him had also got in the way of clear thinking. God knew how acutely aware of him she was in that sense.

They left Holland the following day. There was no way Deborah wanted to stay on any longer and she played down her discomfort as much as possible, though how much she fooled James, she didn't know. He saw to it that she kept off her feet as much as she could—after an initial attempt to persuade her to stay on a few more days. But there was Joan to think about and—and she didn't want to be alone with him in the house any longer.

Maybe she did love him a little, but she wasn't in love with him, which was what she had thought when she'd spoken to him in the middle of the night. No, in the clear light of day she realised her mistake and she was extremely grateful for James' wisdom in not taking her seriously. She was also grateful that he never alluded to the scene which had taken place in the early hours.

When they had been back in Yorkshire for a week everything was back to normal except that squash was out of the question and either James or Mr Ollerenshaw the gardener had to drive Deborah to work for the first few days.

By the third week of July all the invitations to Sir Henry's birthday party had been sent out and he was looking forward to it very much, as was everyone else in Vale House. Two postcards and one letter came from the honeymooners and Louise made several suggestions about the party, like putting lights in the gardens and patio at the back of the house in the hope that it would be a clear evening, like hiring musicians and hiring caterers to help Bessie. But Deborah had already thought of all these things.

James was put in charge of the bar arrangements and the champagne with which Gramps was to be toasted and congratulated on reaching seventy-five.

Gramps didn't mind all the fuss, which surprised both Deborah and James somewhat. They decided he was going along with it all to please his loved ones as much as anything else.

'You're getting a bit carried away, aren't you?' Sir Henry made his first protest, a mild one, one morning at breakfast, when James told him what sort of champagne was to be delivered that afternoon.

Deborah sprang to James' defence. 'James is quite right in ordering the best, Gramps. It isn't everyone who celebrates being ...' she grinned impishly, '... three quarters of a century old.'

His bushy grey eyebrows went up an inch. 'Seventy-five if you don't mind. Putting it the other way makes me sound archaic! And since when do you take James' side in things? And who's going to pay for all this, that's what I'd like to know. Me, I suppose!'

They just laughed at him until he joined in, and when Bessie came in with a pot of tea, she started laughing, too—though she didn't know what it was all about!

'There's a phone call for you, Deborah,' she said, her face wreathed in smiles. 'It's Mr Brown.'

'Denis?' It wasn't like him to ring at eight o'clock in the morning! She took the call on the hall telephone.

His familiar voice came over the line and he sounded very pleased with himself. 'Deborah? I've had good news in the post this morning and—well, I'd like to discuss it with you. Will you have dinner with me tonight?'

'Yes, if you like.' She was intrigued.

'I'll pick you up from home at—eight o'clock?'

'Eight will be fine, Denis, but there's no need to drive all the way out here.' More often than not she met him in the town centre. 'I'll meet——'

'No, no, that's all right. I'll collect you. I'm—taking you somewhere a bit special.'

She was more intrigued. 'Fine. See you this evening.'

When she got back to the breakfast table she told James and Gramps about the call. 'Something's up,' she added, thoughtful, 'he sounded pleased with himself—almost excited, and I've never known Denis to get excited.'

'Is that a fact?' The remark came drily from James.

Deborah's eyes went straight to his and she felt a tinge of colour on her cheeks. Was she reading ambiguity into his words, or was it deliberate?

She glanced at Gramps, but he was tucking earnestly into his breakfast.

CHAPTER NINE

'How was the cricket?'

Gramps looked up from his newspaper, smiling at her fondly. 'You don't really want a blow by blow account, do you?'

'Nope!' Deborah kissed him, as she always did on getting home from work. 'Did James go with you?'

'No, Ollerenshaw drove me and collected me. James has gone out for the day, he told us about it at breakfast this morning, don't you remember?'

'No, maybe it was while I was on the phone to Denis.' Very casually she asked, 'Who's he gone out with?'

'Diane Massey, of course.' He shook his paper a little impatiently and folded it in half. 'Personally I don't know why he sees so much of her. It's every week, isn't it? Sometimes twice.'

'That isn't fair, Gramps. You don't know anything about her except what she does and where she works.'

'Of course I do! I knew her years ago, when James was courting her.'

'Courting her?' Deborah suppressed a smile at the phrase, she also tried to suppress the feelings of alarm which took hold of her. She hadn't realised things had been *that* heavy with James and Diane in the past. He had referred to her more than once as merely 'an old friend.'

'It was before you came to live here,' Gramps went on. 'James was—oh, twenty or twenty-one, I suppose. He saw quite a bit of Diane and he brought her here a few times. She was a pretty thing with a mop of black hair and big blue eyes. Of course he never let her get in the way of his studies . . .'

'Of course.'

Sir Henry's eyes moved swiftly and shrewdly to hers. 'Do I sense a touch of jealousy. Debbie?'

'Don't be silly! Gramps! What a silly idea. What possible difference could it make to me who James goes out with?' Careful now, she thought, your grandfather doesn't miss a thing. She shrugged. 'It was you who didn't seem thrilled at the idea.'

'All I said was that I don't know why he sees so much of her. I can't imagine that she's his type, that's all. Not these days, I mean. She's been married and divorced twice and she has two children, one to each marriage. Mind you, I believe she's damned good at her job—a theatre sister, you know.'

Deborah did know. She was thinking now that Diane Massey obviously had gifts other than professional ones which kept James interested. He had taken her out regularly for some time now. She was coming to the party next week, too, and then Deborah would be able to see for herself what she looked like and what her relationship with James really was.

She poured a drink for her grandfather, giving more thought to Diane Massey than she ever had before. Some time ago, James had likened his relationship with Diane to Deborah's relationship with Denis. What was it he'd said? Something about just keeping each other company.

Denis! Heavens, he was calling for her at eight and she wanted to have a bath and wash her hair. She excused herself from Gramps and went upstairs, pondering over what to wear. He'd said he was taking her somewhere 'a bit special'. Where, exactly? She should have asked him—the venue would dictate what she wore. She had bought quite a few new clothes of late and . . .

And what were James and Diane doing for the whole of the day? Were they spending the evening together, too? It must be Diane's day off. Maybe they'd gone out for a picnic or—or maybe they were spending the day at her house. If so, would her children be there? Of course they would. Deborah smiled with satisfaction—it was Saturday today. Besides, the children were on school holidays now. Of course, that was no guarantee that they were around . . .

It was no use. She couldn't deny to herself that which she had denied to Gramps. She was jealous. As jealous as hell!

She forced James and her jealousy to the back of her mind as she got dressed for her date, switching her thoughts back to Denis and his good news—and trying to keep them on that subject.

Her hair was behaving beautifully and she left it loose, as she did most of the time these days. She changed her undies, put on fresh stockings in a light shade of tan and a beige dress which was sleeveless and cut low at the front. Yes, that would do nicely. It was slinky but simple and would be appropriate for dining almost anywhere.

Denis was fifteen minutes early, which wasn't like him. He was normally punctual to the minute. Bessie came to tell her of his arrival and, with a hasty spray of perfume to complete her preparations, Deborah went down to find him chatting with Sir Henry. Drinking with Sir Henry, in fact.

'Hello, Denis. Sorry I kept you.'

He stood, looking smart in a dark brown suit, white shirt and tie. He didn't look forty-seven; his brown hair had not a touch of grey in it and he had nice eyes, lively eyes. There was little else to be said about him really, except that he was kind and gentlemanly. Of course he wasn't as tall as James and by no means . . .

'Deborah, you look lovely! You haven't kept me, I was early.'

'Will you have a sherry with us, Debbie?'

'Yes, please, Gramps. Shall I pour it?'

'Sit down, lass. I'll get it. I'm not too old to wait on you once in a while.'

She had been in Denis' car less than two minutes when she realised where he was taking her. Disappointment washed over her, but she could hardly complain. 'We wouldn't be going to Luxton Hall, by any chance?'

'Why, yes!' He took his eyes from the road. 'How did you guess?'

'From the directions we're taking and—intuition, I suppose.'

He was a little put out. 'You've spoiled my surprise. Do you know the place then? You've never mentioned going there before.'

Turning to look out of the windows, she said, 'Just once.' Her eyes closed briefly. James. James, James, James ... 'It's very swish, Denis. Your news must be good!' It was an effort to put lightness into her voice. She didn't want to go to Luxton Hall with Denis but what on earth could she do when he was being sweet and giving her a surprise? 'Perhaps this is a celebration? Luxton Hall is the sort of place one might go to for ...'

'Well, I think so, I hope so.' He didn't interrupt her, exactly. She had let her voice trail off. She turned to see him smiling at her a little uncertainly as he went on. 'You see, it rather depends on your point of view.'

Her effort was valiant then. She did her utmost to shake off thoughts of someone else, anything else, and to concentrate on her escort. 'Well now, am I to guess what this is all about, or are you going to put me out of my misery?'

The question seemed to please him for some reason, making her feel guilty at her exaggeration. To be truthful, she wasn't all that interested. Intrigued but not miserable because of her suspense. She watched him looking quite chuffed, like a little boy who'd been given a red star for getting his sums right, and she felt vaguely sorry for him, illogical though that was. 'You've won the football pools, is that it?'

'Deborah, you know I never gamble.' His serious reply made her sigh inwardly. He had no sense of humour; how come she'd never noticed this lack before? Still, he was a good man, a sweet man, and she left it to him to pick the moment when he would reveal all.

Denis' news affected her not one iota but she didn't have to feign a response, she was genuinely pleased for him. He picked his moment in the cocktail lounge, the bar where she had first started to get to know James for what he really was.

'Promotion! Denis, that's wonderful! Congratulations. It sounds like a much bigger branch than the one you manage here.'

'Oh, it is!' He was watching her avidly, drinking in her response. 'It'll be quite a responsibility but I'm up to it.'

'You've earned it. I'm very happy for you, Denis. But how come this is the first I've heard of it? I mean, you must have had interviews or something?'

'I didn't want to say a word until I got official confirmation. I only told the boys today.'

'And what did they say? I mean, moving to Birmingham and all . . .'

'Stevie starts at Liverpool University soon,' he shrugged. 'And John's got two more years to go. It won't affect them.'

'And you? You've lived in Yorkshire all your life.'

'Then it's time I had a change,' he said brightly. 'Another drink? We must drink a toast now I've told you.'

'Yes, of course. When will you be leaving?'

He looked at her strangely then. 'In the middle of September. And Deborah, I'm afraid I won't be able to make Sir Henry's birthday party next week. I'll be spending the week-end down in Birmingham. There are a lot of things I have to sort out—somewhere to live for one thing. I can't leave it too late.'

'I understand. I'm sorry,' she said, and meant it. 'Did you tell Gramps?'

'No, I'm afraid I'm leaving that to you.' Denis looked extremely sorry, as though his absence from the party would make the world of difference to Sir Henry. 'To have told him tonight would have necessitated giving him my reason and——'

'And you wanted me to know first.'

It was a Saturday evening and Luxton Hall was busy, though the only way it showed was in a slightly slower service when it came to being served dinner.

When the waiter came to announce that their table was ready, Deborah's inner disturbance deepened as she and Denis were shown to the very same table she had shared with James, a corner table for two, complete with candles and a single rose in a crystal vase. Had she been able to give a good reason for it, had there been fewer people in the restaurant and thus more space, she would have asked to be seated somewhere else.

It was a dull, lifeless, depressing evening in spite of the luxurious surroundings. But it got far, far worse between the main course and the dessert. That was the moment Denis chose to drop his bombshell, or rather, to take all his courage into his hands.

He approached the question from all angles, hedging and supposing and if-ing and enticing, and Deborah gave him her full attention, wondering what on earth he was leading up to, because she didn't see it coming. She certainly had not expected this!

'Deborah, I've given a great deal of thought ... of course you'll want to think about it, too, but if you'll consider ... I mean, I know how much you love Vale House, but ...'

That was how it went. For minutes. Long minutes before he asked her to marry him.

She couldn't believe it. His hand came across the table to take hold of hers and she looked down at it stupidly as if she'd never seen a hand before.

'. . . be very grateful, Deborah, and proud, if you would do me the honour of marrying me.'

Her heart dropped like a bird shot full of lead in mid-flight. Stunned, she didn't know what to say. Denis—this man with whom she had had an understanding, a man whom she still believed to be in love with the memory of his dead wife, this sweet, kind, undemanding *companion*, was asking her to marry him!

She wanted to cry. Oh, how she wanted desperately to cry. It was more than she could control fully and her eyes filled with tears. She bit hard on her lip as a small, pain-filled sound emitted from her.

Denis' hand tightened over hers. His laughter was short and a little too loud from nervousness. 'I know this is something of a surprise, darling . . .'

Something of a *surprise*! *Darling*! She looked at him, already shaking her head in an effort to stop him saying any more.

'. . . but we've been saving more of one another than we used to. Every week, at your instigation, and I began to hope that—Deborah? My dear, you don't have to say anything yet. Don't say yes and don't say no. Think about it. I know I'm considerably older than you but—well, we wouldn't be the first couple, would we? And if you would like children, I mean, I know how fond you are of children and—and forty-seven isn't too old to start another family . . .

'Of course we'll choose our house together. We can start looking next week-end. That is, if your answer's yes. Perhaps something on the outskirts of Birmingham . . .'

'Denis.' Since he'd actually dropped his bombshell

she had had several minutes in which to think of a response which would in no way hurt his feelings. 'I'm very, very touched,' she said quietly, and of course that was the truth. 'But you know, you should know, that marriage is not for me.'

'But——'

'No, Denis. Please don't make this more difficult for me. You're a fine man and you would give me a good and comfortable life, I know. But you know my views—why, our lack of interest in emotional involvement has been the corner-stone of our relationship. So you know it's nothing personal. I'm just not interested in marrying—anyone.' She should not have added that last word. It was the first time she'd departed from the truth.

But what could she say? I'm not interested in marrying *you*? You see, I'm in love with James Beaumont. I've been denying it to myself ever since I came back from Holland, but I can't deny it any longer. And I *hate* to be sitting here with you, refusing you when you mean so well, while I'm sitting here at this table where I sat with James. In fact all I want to do right now is run away from you. Now, right now. This is the wrong place, the wrong man, the wrong proposal . . .

To her indescribable relief, Denis did not go on. Nor was he depressed. He chose a dessert from the trolley when the waiter approached their table with it and they carried on talking almost as if a proposal had not been mentioned. Almost. Of course Deborah did not show her agitation to get away. She would not hurt him by doing that. But she didn't eat anything else. She finished her wine and had brandy when coffee was served. Two brandies, in fact. And Denis had a couple, too, which was most unlike him considering he'd been drinking wine, as well as two aperitifs, and considering he was driving. Perhaps he wasn't taking her refusal as well as she'd first thought.

He wasn't. It became obvious to her as he got quieter and quieter, and the drive home over the moors was awkward, with Deborah striving to prolong a one-sided conversation. Denis was by no means unpleasant; he just didn't say anything, and yet he was driving slowly, as though he were in no hurry at all to let go of her. Or was he being cautious because he had drunk a little too much?

With a surreptitious glance at her watch, which she couldn't read in the dark, she wished fervently he would put his foot down a little. When they turned into the lane which led to Vale House she felt as though a weight had lifted from her shoulders.

And then it started.

Without a word of warning Denis drew the car to a halt, pulling off the road to park by a copse which was two or three hundred yards from her home. The lamps were sparse along the little-used lane and when he killed the engine and switched off his lights, the only illumination worth mentioning was that of the moon.

'Denis, what is it?' She would have been alarmed had she been with any other man. Well, except for . . .

'I want you to promise me you'll think about marrying me, Deborah.' He held up a hand. 'No, please. I know you've given me an answer but you didn't take time to think.'

Gently, she said, 'Denis, really, I don't need to.'

What he did next was so out of character that she was taken completely unawares. He virtually grabbed hold of her, his arms going around her with alarming strength, pulling her towards him so that his face was inches from hers. 'Deborah, I——' Then he was kissing her, he was kissing her and it was repugnant to her. It was too soft, too wet, and he had all the finesse of a slobbering uncle who had had too much to drink.

She didn't fight him. It was the hardest thing she'd had to do in years, not to fight him and show her revulsion. But this was Denis; he had feelings like anyone else, she had known him a long time and she wasn't going to hurt those feelings with an unnecessarily violent reaction.

That was a mistake. He lifted his head just briefly, just long enough to say, 'Deborah, oh, darling, I want you! I've wanted you for a long time.'

'Denis! What's—*Denis!*'

It got serious very, very quickly. His right hand went up her skirt, directly to the top of her stockings, and then he lost control. His mouth was on hers again, his breath was on her face and she wriggled like an eel, unable actually to fight him because of the way he was holding her. She would never have believed he had this sort of strength; with one arm he held her against the seat of the car, awkwardly, so that her body was twisted against him, while his free hand slid along the bare skin at the top of her thighs until his fingers were edging beneath her panties.

She went berserk. It was anger more than fear which sent the adrenalin pumping through her body and she got one arm free, her head up, and she started yelling at him at the top of her voice, almost sliding to the floor when he suddenly let go of her—whether it was from her own efforts, she couldn't be sure.

Then everything was still, silent except for the sound of their breathing, Deborah's coming to her in painful rasps.

'Deborah, I——' He started shaking his head, looking appalled. 'I'm so—what can I say? I'm so sorry, so sorry. I wouldn't—I mean, you, of all people. I wouldn't hurt you, Deborah. I love you. I——'

'I'll see myself home.' She was already crying. Silent tears. Shocked tears. Sad, pathetic tears. She wouldn't look at him, couldn't look at him.

'No, no, I'll drive you——'

But Deborah was already out of the car and walking.

She walked quickly along the lane towards Vale House wondering, irrelevantly, how long he would sit there in the car. He didn't switch his engine on. The moment she turned into the drive, out of his vision, she ran. She ran as quickly as the gravel crunching beneath her feet would allow her to, gratitude and relief spurring her on as she saw that the house was in darkness. Thank God, thank *God* everyone was in bed!

She let herself in by the back door simply because access would be quieter that way, nothing creaked there and there was no heavy door which needed a firm push to close properly, as the front door did.

It was for the kitchen that she headed, picking her way around the familiar furniture without even switching a light on. She got to the sink and scooped handfuls of cold water to her face. She wasn't crying now, nor was she thinking; she was doing what instinct dictated.

'Debbie?'

The noise which tore from her was between a scream and a squeal and she wanted to die as it was met with low laughter.

'Hey, take it easy, it's me! I haven't been in long myself and I heard your footsteps on the——' James finished the sentence as he switched the light on. 'I didn't hear a car but—Debbie! What the *hell* . . .?'

She could imagine how she looked. 'I'm all right,' she said quickly. 'I'm all right, James.'

He just stared at her, unable to reconcile what he was thinking with what he could see. 'But I—I thought you were out with Denis? Where . . . what . . .?'

'I was. He—dropped me off in the lane.'

James' face changed completely. 'Like hell!' he exploded.

He moved swiftly towards her and she put trembling hands to her cheeks. 'Don't, James, *please* don't be angry, I—I can't bear it just now.' And then she was sobbing, her head resting against his shoulder as he held her tightly, stroking her hair.

The fury in him made his body rigid and he swore as she had never heard him swear before. She wanted to tell him there was nothing to fuss about really, that she didn't know why she was crying like this with tears so very different from the silent ones she had shed earlier. But there was too much emotion inside her and she couldn't give vent to it in words.

The comfort of being held by James was blissfully reassuring. He must have been in his room at the back of the house, about to retire, when he heard her hasty footsteps on the gravel. His black shirt was open to the waist and she breathed in the clean smell of him, dampening his shirt as she cried against his shoulder.

She drew away from him, accepting the hanky he gave her, knowing she must pull herself together. Why was she over-reacting like this? 'I—I'm sorry. There's really no need for me to go on like this. Nothing serious happened and——'

'*That* is a matter of opinion!' he said furiously. He took hold of her wrist and half pulled her towards the drawing room, flicking on the overhead light before he led her to the big mirror over the fireplace. 'Look at yourself. Look!'

She looked awful. Her hair had been tossed all over the show, her mascara had run, there were dried streaks of moisture on her face and one shoulder of her dress was partially torn, the narrow band of material hanging limply against her arm, exposing her bra strap. She looked down at what she couldn't see in the mirror, her gaze following James' to her crumpled skirt, the ladder in her stockings, the dust on her feet and shoes.

'Now tell me nothing serious happened! Tell me you were a willing party to this.' His eyes were black with anger. 'I'll break his *neck*!'

'James!' she gasped. 'James, you don't understand. Denis isn't—he asked me to marry him!'

'What?'

'He——' She broke off, realising what a ridiculous answer that must have been. It was hardly relevant. 'James, please, listen to me. He meant no harm. He was . . . very emotional tonight and——'

'You're *defending* him?' He was incredulous.

'And he'd had a drop too much. Yes, I'm defending him. He just—for once in his life, he lost control. There's nothing more to it than——'

'God in Heaven.' His shoulders dropped as he let out a harsh breath, his hand going to the back of his neck. 'All right. Maybe it's you who's answerable for this!' His eyes went to the swell of her breasts in the low neckline of her dress. 'So he wants to marry you. Did you know he'd been leading up to that? Did you know how he feels about you? Did you realise you must have been driving him crazy for *months*?'

'No! *No!*' She stared at him, unable to believe that his anger had turned on *her*! 'This . . .' She glanced down at herself, wide-eyed as she looked back at him. 'I—I didn't expect any of this. Any of it! I—I would never have believed Denis was like that!' It was her only defence, and it was the truth.

With a short bark of laughter, James' eyes went to the ceiling. He shook his head slowly, looking at her as if she were unreal. 'I once told you, years ago, that *all* men are like that. Debbie, haven't you learned anything at all in the past ten years?'

Fresh tears sprang to her eyes. Her teeth bit into her lower lip and she willed herself not to cry again. Oh yes, she had learned a great deal in the past ten years. But she'd only learned it since the day James had pointed out how little she'd learned!

She had been afraid of the past and afraid of the future. Afraid of loving again. She had functioned as a business woman, though that was not really what she wanted from life. She had lived in a vacuum, a bubble which was safe, without emotional highs or lows. Just safe.

Until James had burst that bubble.

Until she had fallen in love with him.

And now she was vulnerable, wide open to the deepest kind of hurts and desperately, dangerously, vulnerable.

'Go upstairs, Debbie.' James' voice was calm only because he was working at it. 'Go to your room and do something about your appearance. I can't bear to see you looking like this. It makes my blood boil. I can't decide who's neck I want to break now—his or yours.'

'James——'

'Get upstairs. Wash your face.' There was a muscle working in his jaw as he stabbed a finger towards the floor. 'Ten minutes. I want you back in this room in ten minutes. I haven't finished with you yet.'

It didn't occur to her to argue with him, not that there would have been any use. Leaving her clothes in a heap on the bathroom floor, she soaped herself quickly under the shower and pulled on a thick, white towelling dressing gown which covered her from neck to foot. She dragged a brush through her hair and went downstairs, and not once did she stop to think that neither she nor Denis Brown were answerable to the man who was waiting for her.

He was standing by the fireplace, one elbow propped on the mantelpiece. Beside him was an empty brandy glass and on the coffee table by the settee there was a drink for her.

She sat down, saying nothing, and picked up the glass.

It was a full minute before he spoke. He came over and sat about one yard from her on the settee, looking at her with raised eyebrows. 'So what happened exactly? Tell me about it.'

'I—there's very little to it, James.' She floundered. She had been expecting a lecture, not this. 'We went out to dinner and he told me he'd had a promotion at the bank. That is, to a bigger branch in Birmingham and——' She shrugged, explaining how he had gone on to propose, how sweet he had been, how nervous. 'He—got progressively quieter on the way home and I was feeling awful——'

'Awful?'

'Guilty.'

'Why? Why should you? You've told me you've never given him reason to hope for—anything.' The last word was spoken with irony.

'I haven't! Not in any way. Ever. So I—I don't know why I felt guilty. I also felt sorry for him, and I can't really explain that, either.'

James impatiently raked the hair back from his forehead. 'And then your sweet and nervous bank manager, your kindly, platonic friend who never gets excited . . .' He gave her a sideways look, not needing to finish the sentence. 'I don't blame him, I blame you. No, no that isn't . . . Dammit—what can you expect, Debbie, when you go out looking the way you looked tonight? That dress was—I can just imagine what went though his mind when he picked you up here. I can imagine even if you can't! Where have you been all your life? You're on your own in the naïvety stakes, do you know that?'

He went on a while longer, but Deborah said nothing. She had thought her own reaction was uncalled for—but this? From James? He seemed deeply troubled and she couldn't understand it. Unless it meant that he cared . . .

Of course he cared. That wasn't news to her. He had told her he was fond of her.

In the ensuing silence her concern was for James. It occurred to her that she could tell him it was no big deal, just as he had dismissed their ... embraces ... in Holland. But that might be misunderstood as flippancy, and he was in no mood for flippancy. She didn't want to risk anything that would make him angry again.

Instead she reached out to him, tentatively, putting her hand lightly on his shoulder. He stiffened. 'James? Why are you so angry?' She spoke softly, moving closer to him almost cautiously. 'There's no harm done. This really is a storm in a tea cup, you know.'

Nothing. He didn't move, didn't look at her, didn't speak.

Deborah acted on instinct. The tables had turned and she had to coax him out of this—this inexplicable black mood which had descended on him. Never had she seen him like this before. She got off the settee and knelt in front of him, taking his face between her hands. 'James, what *is* it?'

Who reached for whom, the precise details of how they came to be holding each other, she couldn't remember. Suddenly she was in his arms and whether he lifted her on to the settee or whether she moved of her own volition ... that was something else she couldn't be sure of.

Their mouths met in a kiss which was spontaneous and filled with a need which seemed to Deborah to go beyond the physical. She could not get close enough to him, could not get enough of him. This was pure emotion and it excluded sexuality.

But James broke it off and held her away from him. She spoke his name just once, the single word being almost a cry, a plea. A deep, troubled moan was her answer and then he was kissing her again, tenderly this time, tenderly but with a hunger which he kept in check.

Her own hunger, she could not keep in check. With only the slightest encouragement from her lips the kiss changed as she invited his deeper exploration of her mouth. She groaned her encouragement for even more, more, and her hands slid of their own volition from his back to the naked skin of his chest to touch firmly but sensually every available inch of it.

Then she was arching against him, her head moving back as his lips progressed to her neck, her throat. Her arousal was immediate but even through the drugging of her senses, she knew that he was holding back. As he had always held back.

She sought his mouth with her own, keeping her arms around him as she moved back against the cushions. There was no alarm in her now, not this time. She was trembling, hungry for him, needing him as she had never needed any man. It was she who pushed the gown from her shoulders, she who guided his hand to her breast.

'Debbie! Debbie, for God's sake ...' His dark eyes bored into her, questioning, disbelieving. 'You don't know what you're doing!' He wrenched her hands from him, his fingers closing tightly around her wrists so her arms couldn't stray, couldn't move.

It might have stopped there, it might have gone no further if she hadn't looked at him with half-closed eyes, her lips swollen and deepened in colour, parted in silent protest.

It might have stopped there if a small and unintentional movement hadn't opened her gown to reveal her nakedness. But it didn't stop there. James' gaze dropped and moved slowly along the pale skin of her body, from her thighs to her firm, young breasts with their dark pink peaks just waiting for his attentions ... erect, irresistible. 'James. James, please ...'

Even as he reached for her, he denied her. 'No. No. This is—Oh, God, you're beautiful! So beautiful!'

For Deborah there was only pure sensation then, no thought, just incomparable and mindless pleasure as James caressed her and kissed her as he had never kissed her before. His breathing was audible now and he lifted his head to rain kisses over her face, her throat, his hands exploring her slowly, expertly, as though he were more familiar with her body than she was.

When his lips moved to her breasts, she cried out, her mind, her body, spiralling higher and higher to a pitch of excitement from which, for her, there was no turning back.

She touched him in a way that could leave him in no doubt that she wanted him to take her now, *now*. But James was still in control—just. Deborah saw but didn't really register what was happening when his eyes closed briefly and a strange, almost agonised look passed over his features. He was battling with himself, and he won. 'Debbie . . .'

That was all he said; his actions said the rest. He moved away from her almost violently, his breathing laboured, his teeth clenched as though he was angry with the world and everyone in it.

'James?' She couldn't believe what was happening, couldn't believe that he was still denying her. He was standing with his back to her and it was all she could do not to scream at him in accusation.

'It's not on, Debbie, it's just not on!' His voice was barely recognisable and his next words were muttered so thickly, so quietly that she didn't even catch them.

'But . . .' With trembling hands, she covered herself, humiliation flooding over her as she fought with herself not to demand of him an explanation. But how could she ask why he didn't want her? Her pride would not allow that.

Besides, that wasn't true. He'd wanted her, he'd wanted her all right, his body had told her that much. It was just the wrong time and the wrong place, certainly the wrong place. It was two o'clock in the morning and their privacy in the drawing room was hardly guaranteed.

When James walked out of the room, however, she knew she'd been making excuses. There were bedrooms upstairs—his, hers, rooms in which their privacy would be ensured. But he had gone without a word, a single word, leaving her to reach her own conclusions about his behaviour.

His behaviour? Surely it was her own behaviour she should be examining! She closed her eyes, calm now except for the ache inside her. She wanted him and she loved him. She loved him and she wanted him. It was as simple as that. She loved James Beaumont more than she had ever loved anyone in her life. As for wanting him physically—well, she hadn't really known the meaning of those words before, not until tonight.

CHAPTER TEN

EVERYTHING fell into place on the night of Sir Henry's party. That James was not in love with her, Deborah was well aware, and she had never spoken to him of her feelings since the night when she'd sprained her ankle in Holland, when he had thought her to be rambling on confusing gratitude with love.

Pride, and the knowledge that life in Vale House must continue in a normal and pleasant manner, helped Deborah during the week following Denis Brown's proposal. She was adept at concealing her emotions, and neither James nor Gramps suspected that anything was amiss with her. Neither did her mother and her stepfather, when they returned from their honeymoon two days before the party. Of course they were wrapped up in each other, and Deborah was grateful for that and the diversion they created.

But she was suffering. It had got to the stage where she was thinking almost constantly about James, and being in his company was by no means as easy as it used to be. Without being obvious she avoided him when she could. Fortunately she had a valid excuse during the week before the party, while she was busy, to refuse his invitation to the sports centre when it was forthcoming. But that was the only invitation James extended to her because he was busy, too.

At the end of August he was to start an appointment as Consultant Paediatrician at the Sheffield Children's Hospital in Western Bank, in the city centre. It was presumably because of this, probably his having preparations to make, that he spent most of his evenings in the library at home.

Most, but not all.

On the Wednesday during the first week of August he went out with Diane Massey and, on the evening of the party, Saturday, he went out before the guests were due to arrive to collect Diane from her home.

The moment Deborah saw them together, everything fell into place and she realised what a fool she had been to nurture secret hopes that one day James would see her as something other than a friend, a girl he was merely fond of.

Diane Massey walked confidently into the drawing room with her hand linked through James' arm, dressed elegantly in a dark blue evening dress which swirled about her legs as she walked. It was cocktail length, with thin shoulder straps, and with it she wore a slim gold necklace and no other items of jewellery—except her redundant wedding ring.

Sir Henry had described her as a pretty little thing with big blue eyes and a mop of black curly hair. That was not how Deborah saw her. Diane was neither pretty nor beautiful but she was certainly attractive. Her dark hair was short and bubbly, her eyes a deep shade of blue and her figure was slim and beautifully proportioned. She was a couple of years younger than James and she had a ready smile which brought a light into her eyes when it was turned on him—which it was for most of the time.

When a reasonable length of time had passed after she'd been introduced to the other girl, Deborah retreated to the kitchen on the pretext of having something to do. Actually, everything was ready for the arrival of the guests and even as she escaped into the kitchen, the doorbell started to ring.

She stayed where she was, ostensibly checking on things while she tried to compose herself inwardly. What a *fool* she was! What a complete and *utter fool* she was in not realising before that James was having an affair with the nurse! He'd been right in saying she was on her own in the naïvety stakes.

But James had lied to her, and that was something she would never have suspected him of doing. No matter what had happened between them, in the recent or distant past, she had never known him to lie to her. Well, there was a first time for everything, and if Deborah had needed confirmation of the obvious, she got it as the evening wore on.

By nine o'clock the house and gardens were full of laughing, chattering people. The musicians were playing and people were dancing indoors and on the patio, James and Diane included. He was the centre of Diane's attention and he barely left her side. If he wasn't chatting to her then he was dancing with her, laughing with her, holding her close and whispering against her ear.

Deborah felt trapped. No matter who she was talking to or dancing with, her eyes constantly strayed to the other couple. She was hardly aware of the music, hardly aware of the food she ate later, excellent though it no doubt was.

Bessie and the people who had been brought in to help were circulating regularly with trays and drinks, and Deborah did her fair share of work. Anything, anything to keep her eyes and her mind off James and his girlfriend.

It didn't work. She had begun by cursing herself for her own naïvety but as time wore on, her anger turned against James. What rubbish he had talked when comparing his relationship with Diane to Deborah's relationship with Denis! It was so obvious that they did more for one another than keeping each other 'company'. She had never, ever, looked at Denis Brown the way Diane was looking at James, her eyes full of admiration, full of secrets . . .

It was only when a tall, grey-haired man claimed a

dance with Diane that James sought Deborah's company. And even then it was only to say that the party was going well.

She pretended not to see him approach, but she stiffened as his hand closed over her arm. She was wearing a white dress which was sophisticated and flattering, not that he noticed. 'You've done a good job, Debbie. Congratulations.' He didn't even look at her. His eyes were on the room at large ... or on Diane. Deborah didn't even follow his gaze.

'It's Bessie who deserves your praise, not I.'

He looked at her then, smiling. 'I'll see that she gets it. Now, isn't it time you and I danced?'

'Sorry.' She swallowed what was left of the drink she was holding. 'I'm needed in the kitchen now.'

'What?'

'You heard me.' She couldn't help herself. She felt that she hated him, and the last thing she wanted was to dance with him now he had finally, temporarily, lost his partner. He was only asking her because of that, or for the sake of appearances.

'Debbie ...' His hand was on her arm again and she fought with herself not to shrug it away. 'You've been ... well, let's say that I appreciate how busy you've been all week, coping by yourself in the shop and everything, but why don't you relax now? Come on, let's——'

'No, James. Thank you. Actually, I think it's time we brought the champagne out and got down to the speeches. Gramps is looking rather tired.'

By some miracle, Louise chose that moment to locate James and say something similar to him. James excused himself and went to organise the champagne. It was then that Louise noticed the strain on her daughter's face.

'Tired, darling?' She smiled, assuming what James had assumed. 'Did you have no luck in getting someone to help you in the shop today? I did suggest——'

'I know, Mummy. But I didn't try to find someone.' Deborah had already explained to her mother that she would be better off on her own in the shop rather than bringing in temporary help who wouldn't have the first clue.

Joan had been off work with a stinking cold since Tuesday but she had telephoned to say she'd probably be back next week. Poor Joan! She was sorry to be unable to come to the party; she'd been looking forward to it so much. 'Someone who can't answer questions or quote prices or even pack things would be more of a hindrance than a help,' she said to her mother.

Hans joined them, his arm going possessively around his wife's waist as someone tapped Deborah on the shoulder and asked her to dance. It was Sir Henry's general practitioner, who was her GP too, an elderly man who had been a visitor to Vale House for many years.

'Deborah, do you have any objection to dancing with your doctor?'

Not with you, she thought, her smile wry. 'None at all!'

It was her mother and Hans who made the speeches, short ones, which were followed by an even shorter one from Gramps. It was spoken at full voice so it would reach every corner of the crowded drawing room and the hall where a few people were standing, unable to get into the room.

The guests' rendering of 'Happy Birthday To You' would have woken the neighbours had there been any within three hundred yards of the house, and it was during the following hour that the party reached its zenith, that time when everyone seems to be having a final hour of fun before the least energetic start to make tracks for home.

By one o'clock a dozen or so had drifted away and by one-thirty, Gramps had called it a day. It was not so easy for Deborah to escape; she had to stick it out till the end, which, as far as she was concerned, was the time when James left to take Diane home.

After that, she felt what was almost a sense of relief. Almost. She was relieved because they were out of her sight but sick at the thought of what would no doubt happen between them now.

Three hours later the house was silent. The trees outside her bedroom window were motionless in the still, warm night ... and she had not yet heard the sound of James' car coming back.

It was daybreak before she heard it, and her heart lay like a stone inside her. There was no longer room for doubt about his relationship with the nurse. None at all.

How would she cope, now, knowing that which James had lied about? It *was* tantamount to lying, his telling her nothing about this affair. So much for his honesty! But at least he had been principled enough not to make love to her, Deborah, while conducting an affair with Diane. Not that he had wanted to make love to her. Oh, he'd been affected by the heat of the moment last week, certainly, but he'd still resisted her, and things would not have gone as far as they had if she had not given him every encouragement.

Filled with shame and regret, she buried her face in her pillow. How was she going to cope with James now? How could she go on living with him, loving him, hating him, knowing what he must feel for Diane?

She saw things differently in the morning, or rather, the afternoon. She had slept only after a great deal of thinking, self-recrimination and condemnation of James, too.

It was turned noon when she woke and the house was

still silent, not a sound to be heard from any direction.
She looked towards the light streaming from a chink in
the curtains, knowing a feeling of helplessness. But that,
at least, was more tolerable to live with than the turmoil
of painful emotions with which she had battled during
the night.

In the light of day, in the silence of her room, she
realised and accepted there was nothing she could do
about anything. James was not to blame for her loving
him. He had made it clear all along that he wanted her
friendship but nothing more. And why should he have
volunteered what went on in his private life? Especially
when he had no idea of her emotional involvement. He
had had no reason for warning her off more explicitly
than he had.

In the early afternoon she went for a long walk
around her beloved countryside, leaving the house
before James got up. Of course she would not be able to
avoid him for ever, any more than she could envisage
him leaving Vale House to live elsewhere. But it would
be for the best if he did. For her.

Deborah talked to herself solidly, reminding herself
there was nothing she could do but carry on as normal
and, during the week that followed, she managed to do
just that. Joan's cold turned out to be influenza and she
was housebound for another week. This kept Deborah
in the shop for longer hours than she would normally
put in and again, during the evenings, James spent a
great deal of time in the library.

At the end of August he took up his appointment at
the hospital and life settled down to a new pattern. She
saw more of her grandfather and less of James, his
hours at the hospital being by no means rigid. She saw
a change in him which was no doubt attributable to his
new responsibilities, his work as a consultant. He didn't
go to the sports centre at all during September, though
Deborah continued to play squash and various other

games because it got her out of the house; it was something to do.

James became somewhat quieter in his settling down process—but he continued to see Diane. Whether he and she had time to see one another during the day, Deborah didn't know. Nor did she care to find out.

Towards the middle of September she got a telephone call from Denis. He wanted to know if she would go out for a drink with him that evening, and he called her at work, five minutes before she was due to open the shop.

She had had a letter from him a few days after their last dramatic meeting, a letter full of profuse and sincere apologies. She had answered it kindly, wishing him all the best in his promotion—but she had not expected this call.

'I'm leaving town tomorrow, Deborah, and I—I wondered if we could have a farewell drink? For old times' sake.'

At first she declined, suggesting it was surely better to leave things as they stood. There were, she assured him, no hard feelings.

'I hope so,' he said. 'But if that's really the case, surely you've no objection to a farewell drink? We could meet in town, couldn't we? Just for an hour or so?'

She relented, seeing no real harm in it. There would be no danger of her being alone with Denis in a public house, certainly no likelihood of his mentioning marriage again. And she would drive herself home afterwards.

It was eight-thirty when she got home. She had spent just an hour with Denis and it had been a pleasant hour. Nevertheless, it was long enough and she left him with well wishes, parting from him at the corner of the street when they emerged into the semi-darkness and a steady downpour of rain.

After telling Bessie that she didn't want anything to eat, Deborah made her way to the drawing room to see Gramps. He was sound asleep in his chair, the television playing quietly to its unappreciative audience. There was no one else around and James' car was not outside or in the garage.

Deborah helped herself to a drink and sat quietly, her eyes drifting to the aquarium and the beautiful tropical fish Gramps was so fond of. She glanced uninterestedly at the T.V. and then at her grandfather, knowing a sudden urge to sit on his knee and have him put his arms around her. Funny, he had never done that when she was a teenager, but he had when she was older. He still did. Come to think of it, she would never have allowed him to make such a demonstration of affection when she was a teenager. She'd been too much in awe of him to get close to him.

Silently she left the room, carrying her drink, and she settled instead in the privacy of her own sitting room. She switched the record player on and put on Mozart's Concerto number twenty-one. But her thoughts drifted to James. She closed her eyes, thinking how glorious the summer had been, how glorious life had been during the months before she fell in love with him and now . . . now there was only emptiness, hopelessness.

Suddenly he was there. She sensed his presence and her eyes came open to see him standing in the doorway, his eyebrows raised questioningly. 'May I come in?'

With an effort, she snapped out of her melancholy, made a move to switch off the record player. 'If you like.'

He looked tired. He had discarded his jacket and he loosened his tie now, opening the top button of his shirt as he sat down. 'Your grandfather's sound asleep— No, leave the music on. It's good. Just what I need.'

She did as he bade her and they sat in silence. Within minutes his eyes were closed and Deborah watched him.

She wondered why he was here, whether he might possibly have seen her in town with Denis and if so, whether he had something to say about it.

But James said nothing. She sat, uncomfortably aware of him as time moved on and she played the second side of the record. He didn't open his eyes and she assumed he had fallen asleep. She watched him, wishing he had never come back to England even though she knew how stupid it was to wish such a thing.

'But why did I have to fall in love with you?' she asked him silently. 'How did it happen? And when will it fade, this terrible ache inside me? You won't find the answer to that in one of your medical textbooks, will you, James? Even Gramps couldn't answer that one, with all his experience.

'I'm living in limbo but neither you nor he are aware of it. I thought I knew how to cope with rejection but I don't. I've never felt like this before. I see now, in retrospect, that I never loved like this before. I was in love in the past. In love. But I love you, James, I'm not only in love with you, I love you deeply, for the man that you are. But why, *why* didn't you tell me about Diane? Why didn't I see it for myself, for that matter? How could I have thought there was nothing to your relationship with her when on the nights you were with her you never came home before one in the morning, sometimes later?'

'I'll give you a penny for them. Sixpence, even.' His eyes were open. The music had stopped and she hadn't even noticed. James had not been sleeping. He had merely been resting his eyes all the time she had been silently talking to him.

She got to her feet to switch off the record player. 'I was thinking about Denis Brown,' she lied. 'I had a farewell drink with him tonight. He's leaving for Birmingham in the morning and—well, I hope he's happy there.'

'A farewell drink? You had no problems, I hope?'

She smiled and shook her head, feigning a yawn because it was becoming too much to be with James like this. It was . . . bittersweet. A pleasure tinged with pain. 'I'm off to bed, James. Goodnight. Help yourself to the records or——'

'Just a minute, Debbie.' The dark brown eyes were alert and he sat up, waving her back into her chair. 'There's something I want to know.'

She didn't sit down again. She was convinced it was something to do with Denis, and she shrugged. 'Go ahead.'

'You're avoiding me again,' he said bluntly, 'and I'd like to know why.'

She dissembled, telling him he was imagining things. 'We've hardly seen each other during the past month— but that's only because we've both been so busy.'

She withstood the examination of his eyes, his searching gaze, though how she managed it she couldn't be sure. Probably because she had to. How he would laugh if he knew that Little Debbie had fallen in love with him! He would pat her on the head and tell her she'd get over it, just as she had in the past. But she wouldn't. What she felt for James Beaumont was different, very different.

'Is that all there is to it?' he demanded softly. 'I have the distinct impression I've done something to offend. Debbie, about that night, the night Denis Brown proposed to you——'

'I don't want to talk about that night!' She looked away from him, her composure shattered. 'Really, James, I'd have thought you'd have more tact!'

He held up his hands in defence. 'Take it easy. There are things that I want to explain to you. Sit down, please. I want to talk to you.'

'I'm going to bed,' she said firmly. 'There's nothing to explain, and I'd be grateful if you don't bring up that subject ever again! I regret what happened, to say the least, and I've no wish to be reminded of it.'

'Regret?' His face changed. He didn't seem to believe her.

'Of course regret,' she said, forcing calmness into her voice. 'You must bear in mind how upset I'd been that night. I was just—turning to you for comfort, that's all. But it all got out of hand and I'm sure you're aware that I don't normally throw myself at men. Why, you're more like a brother to me than——'

'A *brother*?'

She had to get out of there before she said something even more stupid. Before she let him know of her jealousy by mentioning Diane Massey's name, by accusing him of doing something he was perfectly entitled to do.

James didn't try to detain her again. He was just looking at her with an expression she couldn't begin to interpret, not that she tried to. She forced a smile to her lips as she left the room and closed the door quietly behind her. Peace must reign. Peace must reign in Vale House and in no way did she want to rock the boat or have anyone suspect what she was going through.

CHAPTER ELEVEN

OCTOBER, a cold and very windy month, passed peacefully. Life was on an even keel. Louise and Hans wrote regularly from Holland and it was usually Deborah who answered the letters, glad that things were going so well for her mother.

Business was getting quieter in the shop, though it had not yet reached its lowest point for the year. Deborah was still buying, still keeping a shrewd eye on trade magazines and papers. In her business, one had to monitor constantly what was happening as far as auctions were concerned, and in early November she spotted something which was of interest to her.

She circled the ad, and looked over at Joan, who was reading the local paper. 'Joan, listen to this: "Silver—a set of Old English Hanoverian flatware, in total weighing 172 ounces, a rare George the First marrow scoop by Richard Richardson of Chester; also a selection of Worcester items comprising . . ." Here, read it for yourself.' She handed her assistant the *Antiques Trade Gazette*. 'They're up for auction at the end of next week—in Oxford.'

Joan read the advertisement carefully, nodded and said she'd send for the brochure straight away. 'I think it'd be very worthwhile taking a look at that little lot.' She paused, putting the trade paper down and picking up the local one, her specs sliding down her nose as she laid it flat on the table. 'Now, you listen to this and see what you think . . . "Professional gentleman, widower, aged 44 and lonely, seeks lady of similar age for companionship, outings, wining and dining, and quiet evenings by the fire. Send details of interests." '

She laughed, but her eyes were watching Deborah keenly. 'What do you think? It's the "quiet evenings by the fire" that get me! And he doesn't ask for a photograph with his replies, which I find comforting!'

Only a few months earlier Deborah would have laughed, too. She would have encouraged Joan to answer the advertisement, if that's what she wanted. But not now. She just shrugged.

'I'm serious this time.' Joan spoke determinedly, tapping her hand against the paper. 'I like his style; I'm going to write to him.'

'If you'll take my advice, you won't bother.'

'Why? Do you think it's suspicious, that "quiet evenings by the fire" bit?'

'Not at all,' Deborah said honestly. 'He sounds like a romantic. But we're better off without any of them. Men—they're trouble, Joan. We're better off without them.'

'You mean, *you're* better off without them,' Joan amended, gently. '*I've* yet to find out. I haven't had your experience.'

Experience? What an odd choice of word! It made Deborah sound as though she'd had hundreds of men. Nevertheless, she nodded. 'I hope you never do.'

They were skirting the subject of James, and Deborah didn't want to get any closer to it. Joan was the one person who had guessed what had happened to Deborah on that score. It was not that she had asked; she had too much tact for that. Nor had Deborah volunteered anything; she never volunteered much when it came to her feelings—not to anyone. But Joan knew, if only because it was she who spent so much time with Deborah, hours and hours on end, when the younger girl couldn't maintain an attitude of cheerfulness and normality without occasionally slipping into quiet, frowning thoughtfulness.

'Perhaps I won't bother,' Joan said glumly.

Deborah's head came up quickly; it was unfair of her to influence Joan like this. 'Pay no attention to me. You do what you feel is right for you.' She smiled, 'Shall I say it? . . . "Better to have loved and lost than never to have loved at all".'

Joan's eyes narrowed. 'Are you sure you agree with that?'

'Yes. Yes, I think so. I think that all——' But she didn't get any farther. A customer came in, one of the few tourists who braved Yorkshire in the winter, an American gentleman who greeted them by grumbling about the freezing weather.

It wasn't freezing on the day Deborah left for the auction at a hotel in Oxford. It was thick with snow. It lay deeply, crisply on the ground, but it didn't look as though it would freeze solid. It was in fact a nice day, with the sun shining brightly if weakly from a pale blue sky dotted with only the wispiest of clouds.

It was also the day when her world fell apart.

She had left Vale House very early, without having breakfast, never dreaming that she had seen her grandfather for the last time. She was halfway to Oxford when the clouds started to gather ominously in the sky—thick and dark and foreboding. When she reached her destination it was to discover that the south of England was covered with snow, too, and no doubt the Midlands had had their fair share of it, judging from the clouds she'd seen.

Undaunted, she found a parking place and walked briskly to the hotel. There she had a late breakfast, and she was in the auction room, examining the items to be sold, when the senior hotel receptionist came looking for her.

He was dressed impeccably in a black jacket and pinstripe trousers and he conveyed his message in a neutral voice, not knowing what lay behind it. 'Excuse

me, are you Miss Wilson-Courtney? Ah. I have a
message for you from your assistant. Would you please
telephone your housekeeper at once.'

Deborah was alarmed, naturally, as she followed the
man to a phone from which she could make the call.
That something must be dreadfully wrong for her to be
contacted like this was obvious to her. Even so, for
some obscure reason it didn't enter her head that
something would be wrong with her grandfather. Not
Gramps, who was as strong as an ox in spite of his age.

A hundred thoughts flashed through her mind as she
dialled her home number, from accidents to fires to a
simple warning that she should stay the night in Oxford
because there had been a further heavy snowfall in
Yorkshire.

'Bessie? It's me. What is it? What's ... Bessie!
Bessie!' The housekeeper was crying, and that was
unheard of.

Deborah's hand tightened on the telephone receiver
when she was finally told to come home immediately.
'It's your grandfather. He's—he's had a stroke and he's
very poorly. James found him this morning in——'

'Where is he?' Deborah shouted.

'At the Royal Hallamshire Hospital—Glossop Road.'

'Is James with him now?'

'Yes, yes, it was James who told me to ring you, but I
had to contact Miss Clegg at the shop first to find out
where you were, and she said——'

'I'm on my way, Bessie. I'll go straight to the
hospital.'

Deborah slammed the phone down. There would be
time enough for explanations after she had seen
Gramps. What mattered now was getting to him. She
dashed to the hotel cloakroom for her coat and then
bolted for her car.

Something heavy seemed to be pressing down on her
chest. A feeling of sickness. Fear. If James had

summoned her like this, it wasn't good ... it wasn't good.

The three hours it took her to reach the hospital were the longest of Deborah's life. It was an horrendous drive, not because of the foul weather, not because she was obliged to drive more slowly than she wanted to, but because she couldn't relax, couldn't breathe properly. Her chest was constricted with this sickening fear and she fought not to give in to thoughts of what might be waiting for her when she got to the hospital.

In an effort to maintain control of herself she clocked up the names of the towns as she made her way north on the A43—Brackley, Silverstone, Northampton, where she joined the M1. She also watched the miles ticking by on the meter on the dashboard, reassuring herself of the progress she was making.

Yet she knew, somewhere deep inside her, that she would be too late. Somehow, she knew, but she refused to think about it. Instead she told herself over and over that at least Gramps would have had immediate help from James, that he would have the best possible attention in the hospital.

At the M1 service station in Nottinghamshire she had to stop for petrol. Thank God the roads were passable. Traffic was slower and denser than normal, but that was the only effect of the weather. And it wasn't very far to Sheffield now.

Not knowing her way round the hospital, she went straight to the reception desk. 'Professor Wilson has been admitted with a stroke. I'm his granddaughter. Tell me——'

The eyes of the woman she was talking to moved from Deborah's face to a point beyond her shoulder. Deborah turned to see James.

He didn't speak, he didn't even shake his head. He confirmed what she already knew, at some intuitive

level, simply by opening his arms to her and holding her
very tightly when she walked into them.

She was grateful for the gesture. But she didn't cry.
She felt . . . nothing. Nothing at all.

James led her to the car park and asked for her keys.

'They're in the ignition,' she said numbly, allowing
him to help her into the passenger seat. Nothing seemed
real. There was a ringing in her ears and her face felt
hot, but inwardly she was strangely calm. 'When—what
happened? In layman's terms, please.'

James didn't start the engine for the moment. He
took hold of her hand and she wanted to tell him that
that wasn't necessary, that he should just answer her
questions, that she was not about to fall apart.

'He had a massive stroke, this morning in his
bathroom. I was up early and I'd taken him a cup of tea
and—I found him. He died almost two hours ago.
Peacefully, without pain. You were on your way back
from Oxford then and I—I thought it best to wait for
you at the hospital, knowing that's where you were
heading. I've spoken to your mother and she's taking
the morning flight from Amsterdam tomorrow. All the
arrangements for——'

'Can we go home now?' She didn't need, didn't want,
to hear any more for the moment.

'Debbie . . .' His voice sounded strange. 'I'm so sorry,
so very sorry.'

She nodded. She looked at him. But in truth she
hardly registered anything about him—his distress, his
words, anything. 'We did everything we could, Debbie.
We, the medical profession. But all the knowledge in
the world couldn't save him.'

There was a catch in his voice but she didn't register
that, either. She just nodded again.

The following days were strange ones, hazy ones. They
were days she thought she would never forget, but later,

after a funeral attended by nearly two hundred people—ex-students, ex-colleagues, friends and neighbours—Deborah came to realise that in a way she had not really lived through those days, not fully. Tablets had been given to her by her GP, tablets which James encouraged her to take.

Presumably she had slept a lot, which was why whole chunks of those days seemed to be missing. Certainly she had wept a lot. It seemed that James had been by her side constantly, though of course he couldn't have been there all of the time.

Bessie, Louise, Hans, the gardener—she remembered talking to them all. She remembered the stream of visitors to the house, the cards and letters of condolence, yet it was all tinged with unreality, as though she had watched the proceedings rather than lived through them personally.

Louise and Hans went home three days after the funeral, by which time Deborah had returned almost to normal. Over breakfast, they urged her and James to join them for Christmas in Amsterdam, suggesting it would be a good idea for them both to be away from the house at that particular time.

Neither James nor Deborah committed themselves. She went to work after seeing her parents off, knowing that she had to some time. Besides, it would be good for her.

In the evening, she broke down again and sobbed after feeding Gramps' fish. James hadn't got home yet and Bessie was out of earshot, thankfully. At length she pulled herself together and found something to do. She was in the utility room, cleaning several pairs of shoes, when James found her.

'How are you?'

'I'm all right, James.' She gave him a smile to prove it. 'If you want any shoes cleaned, stick them on there.'

'You might be sorry you said that!' He returned her

smile but his dark eyes were not amused. He was watching her closely. 'I'm worried about you, Debbie.'

'There's no need.' She carried on with what she was doing. 'You can hardly expect me to be joyous, can you?'

'Of course not.' He leaned against the freezer, tiredly running a hand through his hair. 'But it's time we talked, Debbie. High time. Will you come——'

'No!' Her voice came out more sharply than she intended. The trouble was that she was no longer sure how she felt about James. The were moments, like now, when his presence was . . . unwanted. All she wanted at the moment was to be left alone. It had even crossed her mind that she could tell him to leave now—for good.

Then again, there were periods during each and every day when she felt certain she would go to pieces if James were not around. It was all so confusing, so confusing. Therefore the wisest thing was surely not to talk to him in any depth about anything.

'I'm sorry. I didn't mean to bite your head off but—but just leave me alone for the time being. All right?'

'All right.' He didn't question her. He didn't ask how long the 'time being' meant. He left her alone, knowing she could seek him out if she needed him. He wasn't going anywhere.

A few days later Deborah got a phone call from her grandfather's solicitor and friend, Max Lawrence. He tried to sound businesslike but his tone was apologetic. 'It's about Henry's will, Deborah. It's—well, it is a matter that has to be dealt with. I've—waited until you were feeling better. I've already spoken to your mother and I've written to her about Henry's bequests and instructions. Now, as far as—in short, may I come to the house tomorrow? It's Sunday tomorrow, is James likely to be home in the afternoon? I—it's not easy to reach him——'

'Max, tomorrow will be fine. I'll tell James. Don't

worry, and please don't apologise. You have your job to do and there's no need for embarrassment. Gramps' will has to be dealt with, and that's that.' She spoke kindly, unperturbed by the subject. 'I should imagine you'll want Bessie to be here, won't you?'

'Indeed, yes. And John Ollerenshaw.'

'Fine. Shall we say three o'clock?'

'Yes, thank you, Deborah.'

Max turned up promptly at three o'clock the next day. Bessie showed him to the library, where the gardener, James and Deborah were assembled.

When the bequests to the long serving gardener and housekeeper had been read out, the two departed, leaving James and Deborah to hear the other details of Gramps' will.

The whole scene seemed distasteful somehow, like a set from a black comedy on which mourning relatives gathered, ears pricked, looking from one person to the next and back to the family solicitor, waiting to hear who gets what.

Of course it wasn't at all like that, but there was a shock in store for Deborah which left her open-mouthed, floundering and at a loss to understand. *'What?'* She stared at the solicitor in disbelief. That she and James were equal beneficiaries financially came as no surprise to her—but *this?* That Gramps had treated both her *and* James as heirs ... 'Would you mind repeating that, Max? In plain English!'

Max showed his embarrassment by coughing. 'Vale House has been left to you jointly, Deborah. This property now belongs to you and James.'

'I don't believe it!' Her eyes went accusingly to the man by her side. James looked at her from an impassive face and he said not a word.

'But Gramps *knew* how much I loved this house! It's my home. *My* home. I never——' She caught hold of herself. This had nothing to do with Max, and her behaviour in front of him was appalling, and embarrassing for the man. 'I'm sorry. Carry on, please. Or is that it?'

There was another cough. 'Er—no. There's a codicil to the effect that both you and James are to live in this house for a minimum of nine months of each year, any nine months, for the next three calendar years. Then and *only* then are you at liberty to sell the property if you wish to. And——'

'There's more?' She couldn't believe her ears! What on earth had possessed Gramps to do this? 'This can't be right! It can't be legal to——'

'It's legal.'

'But——'

'Let me finish, please, Deborah. If you want to discuss things with James later, that's up to you, but it is my job to see that Henry's instructions are carried out precisely. Now where was I . . . Ah, yes. Should either of you fail to meet this proviso, that is to say if one or the other of you lives elsewhere for more than three months of each year during the next three years, that person relinquishes ownership and all claim to the property to the other. Is that clear to you both?'

Deborah looked at James in time to see him nodding slowly. There was a wry smile pulling at his mouth, and it infuriated her beyond description.

'You might well smile, James. Gramps has tied it all up very neatly, and it suits you, doesn't it? Well, it doesn't suit me. I intend to fight this!'

'You'd be wasting your time.' The warning came from Max.

'But my grandfather can't——'

'He can. He has. He was perfectly entitled to——'

'When was this will made out?' she demanded. 'When is it dated?'

'I read that out to you, Deborah.' So he had. It had been made out in June of that year. 'I'm sure Henry knew exactly what he was doing. The codicil was an afterthought, but a carefully considered one.'

James spoke for the first time, an oblique remark which did nothing to pacify Deborah. 'Henry always knew exactly what he was doing.'

'Is that all you have to say?'

'Yes, Debbie. That's all I have to say. For the moment,' he added pointedly.

Max moved his briefcase from the floor to the desk, standing.

'Just a minute, Max.' Deborah got to her feet, too. 'What happens if we *both* break the rules—simultaneously?'

The solicitor looked at her gravely. 'I put the same question to your grandfather.'

'And?'

'And he just smiled. He smiled and said that that was purely hypothetical, that it wouldn't happen. I advised him to cover the contingency—and he told me not to fuss, to take it from him that one way or another you and James would each live in this house for at least nine months of each year, and so on. After three years, you're free to do as you wish.' He finished with a shrug, closing his briefcase with a touch of finality. 'Well, goodbye for now. Both of you. I'll—see myself out.'

They let him do just that.

The library door clicked shut and Deborah turned to find James grinning from ear to ear. She felt as though she were about to burst into flames, it angered her so. And it certainly precluded any reasonable conversation they might have had.

She set about him with a vengeance. 'Satisfied, are you? You think it's funny that I haven't got a home to call my own?'

'Don't be silly. You've got——'

'You! I'm stuck with *you* for most of the next three years—or I have to give up this house to you!' She

threw up her hands in horror at the thought of losing
Vale House. Equally disturbing was the idea of being
trapped in the house with James, in this—this
nothingness of a relationship they had! She would end
up hating him. Him—and all the women he would
bring home. It was impossible, the whole situation was
impossible!

'*Stuck* with me?' All trace of amusement left his eyes.
'Don't you see what's behind all this, Debbie? Don't
you see that Henry——'

'I'll tell you what I see,' she shouted, pointing at him.
'I see a man who's been treated for far too long like a
member of the family. I see a man who's not entitled to
live in this house, never mind own it!'

'Debbie, Debbie, calm down. You're not yourself at
the moment, you're still suffering from the shock
of——'

'How *dare* you!' She glared at him. 'I'm not
suffering from anything. I'm not as stupid as you take
me for, James Beaumont. I'll tell you what's behind
all this—*you*! Oh, you timed it well, didn't you,
coming back to England when you did, so you could
wheedle your way back into an old man's emotions
—and into his will! You came back when Gramps
was getting old and you knew he couldn't have had
many years left. After all, you knew about his first
stroke and——'

'That's enough!' The words came quietly, but very,
very, sharply. Then, his eyes closing briefly, he added
almost gently. 'If this is what you see, I'll leave.'

'What?'

James didn't look at her as he got to his feet. 'I said
I'll leave. This business can be very easily resolved, if
you'll just think about it. I know what Vale House
means to you, Debbie. Well, it's yours.'

'Mine?'

He shrugged, bringing his eyes back to her

disbelieving stare. 'Yes, all yours. All I have to do is leave. It's as simple as that.'

'What ...? When?' She didn't believe him. She blinked in confusion. 'Do you mean now? Today?'

James looked at her sadly, making a move towards her, an arm outstretched to her. 'Debbie, please sit down and listen to me.'

She stepped away from him, her hand going to her temple where a slow throbbing was causing a pain over her eye. 'Just answer my question,' she snapped.

James stopped in his tracks. He turned and headed for the door. 'Think, Debbie. Try to be practical. Of course I can't leave today. I'll leave in the new year—after Christmas.' He paused as he opened the library door. 'I'm going out for a couple of hours. There's a little boy I want to check on at the hospital. Bessie's in the house if you need anything. If you'll take my advice, you'll lie down and rest for a while.'

She did nothing of the sort. She sat down, trying to think, a process which was not aided by the headache which was taking over. Would he really leave? Vale House ... Gramps ... James ... her mind was tumbling in confusion with all of these things.

At length she realised she would have to give in and take some tablets for her headache. She was crossing the hall, heading for the bathroom, when the doorbell rang.

She opened the front door to find Diane Massey standing there, looking pleased with herself.

'Yes?' Deborah spoke sharply, her eyes going to the small package which the other girl was holding.

'Is James at home? No? Oh.' She seemed very disappointed and not at all put off by Deborah's attitude. 'Well, not to worry. Would you mind giving him this, please, Deborah? And a message ...'

If she thought she was going to be invited in, she was wrong. Deborah took the box, nodding curtly.

'. . . Would you tell him that . . .' Diane paused, smiling to herself, seeming to be hunting for the right words. 'Tell him that this is a memento of yesterday.' She laughed a little, her deep blue eyes shining. 'And tell him I'll be eternally grateful—I hope!'

Dear God, Deborah thought, have I now to pass lovers' messages and gifts to and fro? Perhaps this woman would like to move in with me and James, until he finds his own place in the new year? Her, and her two children.

Sickened, she stepped away from the door and closed it with barely a nod in the other girl's direction. She looked at the box. It was small, made from cardboard, shiny, gold cardboard, and it had been sealed at the edges with thin strips of tape. It was something small and expensive, judging by the look of it.

She gritted her teeth, furious with herself for not telling *Ms* Massey to deliver her own messages and presents. If she hadn't been so taken aback at seeing her, she'd have said just that. And what the hell was that supposed to mean: 'Tell him I'll be eternally grateful—I hope!'?

She took the box into the library and slung it on the desk. A moment later she was scribbling a note to James, knowing, now, precisely what she was going to do. She wrote down the message and restrained herself from adding her own facetious remark to it. Instead she went on to say that she was going to Amsterdam immediately and would be staying there until he vacated the house. Would he please ring her and tell her what date that would be. She signed the note 'Deborah'.

Next, she went in search of Bessie, who was having a nap in her room. She didn't disturb her. Instead she went into her own room and quickly packed to capacity her two biggest suitcases. Only then did she make her enquiries about flights to Amsterdam. She put down the phone, strumming her fingers against the receiver. Bother! She couldn't get a flight out until tomorrow.

Determined not to be in the house when James came home, she put her cheque book and passport in her handbag and put it, herself and her suitcases into her car.

She had to see Joan, to pay her in advance, to give her instructions and to explain as little as she could get away with explaining. And Joan, she knew, would be only too happy to put her up for the night.

CHAPTER TWELVE

'*DEBORAH!*' Louise did not seem pleased to see her daughter, not at first. She was—shocked.

'I'm sorry to descend on you like this.' Deborah felt like crying. Here she was, a twenty-six year old woman, standing on her mother's doorstep like a lost waif, her teeth chattering against the cold. She felt about three years old. She looked down at her suitcases then up at her mother.

'Oh, darling, come in, come in! You look so cold, so tired ...' Louise effectively blocked her daughter's entry by moving on to the top doorstep then, her head going from side to side as she glanced along the road. 'Where's James?'

'James isn't with me. He——'

And then Hans appeared, beaming, welcoming as he reached for the suitcases. 'What a lovely surprise! You're here for Christmas—yes?'

'I——' She couldn't blame him for grinning. Christmas was three weeks away.

'Hans, I'm sorry——'

'Where's James?' Now he, too, was looking expectantly for the appearance of the man who wasn't there.

'Deborah's alone, darling.' Suddenly she was being hugged by her mother, ushered inside with promises of tea and warmth and food and—oh what a lovely surprise this was ... But was anything wrong?

'Not really.' It was a silly thing to say in the circumstances. Of course something was wrong. Why else would she drop in out of the blue—from another country—without so much as a phone call by way of warning?

170

Still, Louise's question had been equally silly. Everyone knew that something was wrong but, in view of Deborah's evasive reply, neither her mother nor her stepfather pressed her for an explanation.

She was fed and she was fussed-over and it was not until the following day, after a long and much-needed sleep, that she talked to her mother about the business of Vale House. Or rather, she tried to.

At the mention of her father's name, Louise started to weep. It lasted only a few minutes, and then she began to talk about him. So did Deborah. She, too, began to weep. It was, she supposed, inevitable. Gramps, dear, dear, Gramps! His death was too recent to be referred to without the interference of emotion.

'You must have read the article in the Sheffield newspaper, Deborah? Wasn't it beautiful!'

'The obituary? Of course I did.'

'No, no.' Her mother brightened. 'The one James wrote. Well, I mean the interview he gave. What a tribute it was to Henry!'

'I never saw it,' Deborah said dully.

'I've kept a copy of it, naturally. I'll show it to you. I can't understand your not having read it, darling. Still,' she added sympathetically, 'you haven't been at all well since . . . The shock, it was a terrible shock for all of us, of course. But for you——'

Hans chose that moment to come into the room. He had been working in his study all morning. Whether he'd actually had things to do or whether he had tactfully left mother and daughter to talk alone, Deborah couldn't be sure.

He looked from one to the other and made himself comfortable without interrupting the conversation.

'You're so lucky,' Louise went on, 'so lucky to be living with James. He's a wonderful man, isn't he? Wonderful!' She was smiling now, her eyes almost sparkling now that James was the topic. 'The way he coped with everything for us. Well, for me, I suppose. I was so grateful to him for making all the arrangements and organising ... Ah, well. That's the sort of man James is. Capable and strong. You'll appreciate his company more than ever now, won't you? And didn't Daddy handle everything fairly? I thought it was so clever of him!'

She looked at her husband. 'I've said this to you, haven't I, darling? How clever Daddy was, how fair he'd been.'

'Fair?' Deborah didn't really need a fuller explanation of her mother's remarks. It had become very obvious that she would get no sympathy here for the plight she'd been plunged into.

'About the house, of course.'

'You—don't feel that it should have been left to me? I mean, just me. I mean, now you're married and ...' She had begun her question casually, and her voice trailed off. From the look on Louise's face, she had accepted her father's dealings as natural, even predictable.

'I think that would have been grossly unfair, Deborah. You know Henry always treated James as if he were a son. The son he never had,' she smiled, casting a flirtatious glance in her husband's direction. 'Look, what he got instead!'

'Thank goodness!' It was the first time Hans had spoken.

'And how sentimental of him!' Louise went on, again referring to her father. 'His wanting to make sure that you and James both stayed on in the house for at least three years!'

'You—think that was sentimentality?' Deborah could feel her stepfather's eyes upon her, but she asked the question of her mother. Surely Louise had known the workings of her father's mind better than anyone?

'What else, darling?'

'Well, I—it could prove to be an awkward situation, don't you think? I mean, the way Gramps has virtually tied our hands. Supposing one of us wanted to marry?'

'Marry? But neither you nor James have wedding bells on the horizon!'

'I don't know what James' plans are.'

Louise had to consider the point now. 'Mm. I—suppose you have a point.' She laughed suddenly, her eyebrows raised questioningly. 'You haven't had a proposal lately, have you?'

Yes, Deborah thought. An unwelcome one, but yes. 'No. You know me.'

'Quite. Marriage lost all its enchantment for you long ago.'

'Perhaps,' said Hans, 'Deborah had never met the right man.' He was still watching his stepdaughter closely.

'Perhaps,' Louise conceded.

Deborah said nothing. Her question had not been answered. What happened if either she or James wanted to marry? Gramps hadn't thought of that. Still, it was academic now. James was leaving Vale House in January next year and by the end of April, or thereabouts, it would belong solely, legally, to her.

One thing was for sure. This conversation was pointless. She had never been particularly close to her mother, and things were no different now. There was no way she could pour out her heart to her mother, or tell of the confusion in her mind, the ambivalence of her feelings for James, her fear that he really would leave Vale House and her fear that he wouldn't.

She couldn't tell Louise that James was having an affair with his 'old friend', that she couldn't bear to see it happening under her very nose. That she loved James. That she hated him for doing this, and she had no right to hate him because he didn't know he was hurting her.

What a mess she was in! What was she going to *do*?

And why, *why* had Gramps complicated matters like this?

'What about some lunch, Louise?'

'Yes, what about some lunch, Mummy?' She was far from hungry but she was grateful for a complete change of subject.

Louise laughed. 'All right. Give me a moment. I was just about to ask—Deborah, you are staying till Christmas, aren't you?'

'Actually, I'm—I'm not sure . . '

'But James will come over then. It was silly of me to assume he was with you yesterday, come to think of it. He must be very busy at the hospital. They always are. But he'll have some time off at Christmas, surely?'

'Yes, but——'

'Well, then!' Her mother stood up, satisfied that the next month of her life was nicely mapped out.

If only Deborah could think the same.

'I'll give you a hand, darling.' Hans followed his wife from the room.

What her stepfather said to her mother in the privacy of their kitchen, Deborah would never know. But something had been said, that was for certain, because afterwards, for Deborah's remaining days with them, no more questions were asked of her. She still hadn't said why she had arrived so prematurely for the Christmas invitation she had never in fact committed herself to. Nor was she asked. About that or anything else.

It had been a mistake, coming to Holland, not only because she was unable to talk to her mother but also because Amsterdam was full of memories.

On the third day after her arrival Deborah experienced a dramatic intensifying of the dull, gnawing ache which lived inside her. That was the day she went outdoors.

She was alone and she was on foot, and everywhere she looked, there were memories of the beautiful week she had spent here with James. She walked past the houseboat where they had had dinner with Brigitte Hinze and her curious assortment of friends. Looking up, she saw the spire of the Westerkerk, the church where Rembrandt was buried—just one of the many places she'd visited with James.

Even the bedroom she was sleeping in gave her no escape from thoughts of him. It was in there that she had told him, deep into the night, that she loved him.

She tried to busy herself by helping her mother around the house, but the house was spotless and Louise was one of those people who preferred to do things her own way in the kitchen. For someone who had had a housekeeper all her life, she had adapted very well indeed. She pursued her own interests, too, her painting in particular. Twice she left Deborah on her own while she went off somewhere or other for a painting lesson.

Hans was at the university for three or four hours each day, working on examination papers, he said, and he invited Deborah to make use of his study in the house, which was crammed with history books, many of which were in English—many of which were about England.

She spent a portion of every day in Hans' study, not because she was interested in his books but because this was her stepfather's room, his private domain, and in there there were no memories of James.

'Darling, I forgot to show you this.' On the Saturday, several days after her arrival, Louise woke her daughter with a cup of tea at ten o'clock, as she had every morning. Today she brought in a newspaper, too, one that looked very familiar. 'It's that article—you know, the interview James gave about your grandfather.'

She dropped it on the bed as Deborah sat up, still

chattering. 'I forgot to show it to you before, but that's hardly surprising, is it? There's so much to think about just now what with Christmas and—oh, I'll have to get down to my Christmas shopping! How many days are there left? It's just over two weeks now, isn't it?'

'Er—yes, I suppose it is.'

'Anyway, right now I'm going shopping for food! I've given Hans his breakfast, and you can help yourself when you get up. All right, darling?'

Alone, Deborah picked up the paper and started to read the article. It was accompanied by a photograph of a younger-looking Gramps and a newly-qualified doctor, James Beaumont. It had been taken after a graduation ceremony at the university in Sheffield and the two men stood close together, their arms around each other's shoulders, both looking as pleased as punch.

She dropped the paper and covered her face with her hands as shame and horror flooded over her. Dear God, what had she done? What had she *done*?

The photograph, the tribute James had made to Professor Sir Henry Wilson, his praise for the older man, the respect for him implicit in every word James had spoken to the newspaper reporter, were all evidence of that which she had never really doubted for one second. This, the love of one man for another, touched her now more deeply than it ever had before.

'Oh, James!' she whispered aloud. 'James, James, forgive me! *Forgive* me!'

She didn't cry. She had shed too many tears already, selfish tears. How concerned she had been about *her* loss, never pausing to think about James' loss, never pausing to consider his distress, his pain, his grief.

She had been so concerned for herself. Self, self, self! It was she who had demanded everyone's attention, she who had broken down under strain, she who had expected all the comforting. Not once, not once had she stopped to think of what James had been going through.

And it was he who had given her all the attention and care she had expected, needed. It was James who had held her when she cried, James who had been there when she woke from bouts of fitful sleep, James who had encouraged her to eat, and tried his best to create diversions for her in an effort to restore a semblance of normality.

There was no haze now. No days tinged with a sense of unreality. Everything was sharp, everything remembered. And how had she repaid the man whose pain had been equal to her own? With the most disgusting insults she could think of.

She flung the covers from the bed and walked quickly to the bathroom. She had to go home. Now. To apologise. Nothing else mattered. She had to go quickly, for if she allowed herself to dwell on the terrible things she had said to James, she would lose her nerve and find herself unable to face him ever again.

'Hans!' She was breathless when she walked into the kitchen, having flung everything rapidly into her suitcases. 'I haven't time to expain this but—I'm going home now. I know there's a flight this afternoon and all I can do is pray I'll be able to get on it. Will you take me to the airport? Now! I shall just wait there for as long as it takes me to get a seat—on any flight to England.'

She expected a bombardment of questions, which would have been fair enough. Instead, her stepfather merely smiled. He walked past her, through the dining room and into his study.

Deborah followed him, at a loss to understand his silence. 'Hans? What are you doing? Look, some other time I'll explain——'

'I'm writing a note to your mother. Go upstairs and get my brown jacket from the wardrobe. I'll get you to the airport as soon as I can.'

For several seconds she just looked at him stupidly. He didn't respond in any way. His head was bent as he wrote.

She came downstairs to find him waiting by the front door, her suitcases by his side. 'Come on, dear,' he said. And that was all he said.

Hans didn't go into the airport building with her. He left the engine of his car ticking over while Deborah found a trolley on which she could put her cases. By now she had realised that her stepfather knew her far better than her mother did. At least, he knew something that Louise didn't know.

She hugged him very tightly, very gratefully. 'It seems that I don't need to explain anything to you, Hans.'

He considered that for a moment, only slightly amused. 'Not that which is most important to you. As for the rest of it . . .' He smiled. 'But then the rest of it doesn't really matter, does it?' He kissed her on both cheeks, his eyes twinkling. 'At least you won't misunderstand me when I tell you I've been wishing all week that you'd go home!' Then, seriously, he added, 'Go along with you. James needs you, Deborah, he needs you more than you realise.'

CHAPTER THIRTEEN

'JAMES needs you, Deborah . . .'

Oh, if only that were true! If only he needed her, *her*, now and forever. But Hans had been thinking only of the present time, and even so he was wrong. James was strong, a strong, complete man who didn't need anyone in particular. Especially her.

She tormented herself with these thoughts, with wishes that things could be different, all the time she was airborne. She had been lucky this time; she had been in time for the flight direct to Manchester's Ringway Airport and there had been a seat available.

Two hours. As the plane circled the airport, she was thinking ahead to the time when she would reach Vale House. With luck, she would be through customs and back in Sheffield in two hours. She looked at her watch. She would be home in time for dinner. What kind of reception would she get? Would James be in? If so, would he be alone . . .

With a little difficulty, Deborah collected her car from the long-term car park. She couldn't even remember which level she had left it on. What a state she had been in, looking back! It was a wonder she had managed to drive herself to the airport in the first place.

She fired the engine, grateful that the car started without any trouble. Surely James would understand, when she explained that she hadn't been thinking straight? He had to, he just had to, because if he couldn't forgive her, she would never be able to forgive herself for all the vile things she had said to him. She was filled with self-loathing.

Please God, she prayed, don't let James loathe me, too.

He was at home. His home. Vale House. His car was in the garage at the back of the house. The garage door was open and she spotted James' car with relief as she drew to a halt.

The kitchen door was thrown open even before she had reached it, by a very anxious-looking housekeeper. 'Deborah! Oh, it's so good to see you. The way you took off like that——' Bessie's frown had already cleared as Deborah stepped into the light of the kitchen. 'But you're better, I can see that! You were so unwell, James said so, not that I needed to be told——'

'Where is——' She broke off to hug the elderly housekeeper who had been so good to her for so many years. 'What about you? How are you?'

'Just fine! But I can't get used to cooking only for one.'

'Well, tonight, at least, you're cooking for two. I'm famished!' Deborah laughed at the look of pleasure on Bessie's face.

'Dinner will be at least an hour, I'm afraid. James has only just got home from work, and he never eats straight away. Shall I make you——'

'No. I'll wait. I shall be glad of an hour with James before dinner, in any case.' She glanced at her watch as she made her way to the library. James had only just got home from work, Bessie said. Heavens, he'd had a long day.

That became obvious when she found him asleep. He wasn't in the library, he was in the drawing room, in Gramps' armchair by the fire, a real, honest to goodness fire. It added cosiness and colour to the room, which was why Deborah had never closed off the fireplace, even though they had central heating.

She looked at him, sleeping. She looked around the room at everything which was dear and familiar to her, then her eyes came back to James. He was more important, more dear to her than anything in the world. How she loved him! Oh, how very, very deeply she loved this man!

James' black lashes flickered open and he looked up to find her watching him, her name barely audible on his lips. 'Debbie . . .'

'James,' she whispered. 'James, I'm so . . . so sorry.' She could hardly get her words out, she was so choked with emotion. Her heart was bursting with love for him and although she had vowed fervently that she wouldn't weep, that's just what she was doing.

And then he was on his feet and he was holding her close, crushingly close, his lips nuzzling against her hair. 'Oh, my darling I've missed you so much. So much! You'll never know . . . I love you, Debbie. I love you more than words can say.'

She leaned against him, her eyes closing as the tears ran down her cheeks. How kind he was, even now! Even now he was being supportive, telling her that he loved her when really he meant only to convey that he was fond of her.

'James . . .' She eased herself from his arms, putting a finger to his lips as he started to tell her again how much he'd missed her. 'Can you possibly forgive me? Can you ever forgive me for the terrible things I said to you? I hurt you so much, I—I can't begin to——'

'Ssh, darling. Come here. Come here and let me hold you.'

Her tears stopped. She had to be strong now. She must say what she had planned on saying, all that she had rehearsed over and over on the plane from Amsterdam. In a moment, she would, but for these few seconds she would enjoy the nearness of him, the strong warmth of his body against hers, the familiar, masculine smell of him. She would revel in all of this and pretend, just for these few seconds, that he really loved her as she wanted him to love her.

'James, I must talk to you . . .'

He didn't let go of her. He just smiled, the dark brown eyes moving hungrily over her face. 'I tried for weeks on end to talk to you, Little Debbie, so you can damn well wait till I'm ready to listen!'

Then he was kissing her. He was kissing her as if there were no tomorrow, and Deborah's mind spun crazily. Little Debbie, he had called her. But he was kissing her hungrily and with nothing, *nothing* held back. On the contrary, his hands had slid inside her coat and were roaming her body, sending delicious waves of excitement tingling along every nerve. 'James!' She couldn't believe what was happening. He *wanted* her. Here. Now. Right now!

She had wondered what sort of reception he would give her—but this? It couldn't be . . . surely he didn't mean what he had told her a few minutes ago?

'You're right.' His smile was wry as he held her away from him. 'First things first. It might be an idea if you take your coat off.'

When she didn't move, he looked perplexed. 'Debbie? Darling, you have nothing in the world to worry about.' He was looking down at her, now looking as if he personally had all the worries of the world on his shoulders. 'Your words last week . . . you didn't hurt me. I knew you weren't yourself. I tried to explain that to you but you wouldn't believe me. You were still in shock and——'

She held up a hand. 'I know. I know it now. But—— James, are you all right? Are *you* all right?'

'No.' He shoved his hands in his pockets and she saw tension creep into the set of his broad shoulders. 'No, actually I'm not. I—I need you to . . .'

'What? You need me? You need me to what?' She held her breath.

'I need you to tell me you love me, Debbie. I need to hear you say it as you once said it before. Just once you said it before, but then, at that particular time, I couldn't be sure that you meant it as I wanted you to mean it.'

'James ...' She closed her eyes, flinging herself blindly into his arms. 'Oh, James, I do love you. I loved you then and I've never stopped loving you. I'll never stop loving you.'

It was a while before Deborah could make sense out of all that was happening, all that had happened not only in the last few weeks but also in the last few months. It was only when James reluctantly stopped kissing her again, when she had discarded her coat and was sitting by the fire, facing him, that everything became clear to her.

'You never spoke of love after we came back from Holland, Debbie. I wanted it to be true, when I heard you say the words, but I could by no means be sure that you meant it. And afterwards ... afterwards, you were cool with me. I was convinced you regretted what you'd said, that it was something you'd murmured on the spur of the moment, after your accident, when you could easily be confusing gratitude with love. That's why I—I never referred to that night. I didn't want to embarrass you for saying something you hadn't meant.'

'Hadn't meant? But—but if I was cool towards you, it's because—because you rejected me. Surely you can see that?'

'Rejected you?' He didn't seem to know what she meant.

She lowered her eyes. 'You warned me off in Holland. And you rejected me here, in this room, the night Denis Brown asked me to marry him.'

He groaned, shaking his head as he realised she was talking about physical rejection. 'My darling girl, you can't have thought I didn't want you!' He laughed humourlessly. 'Have you no idea what it cost me to keep my hands off you—to *try* and keep my hands off

you? I didn't do too well, did I? I had to call a halt,
Debbie, I had to. One more minute of that and I'd have
made love to you right there on Henry's settee. Don'
you see, darling? You are *Henry's granddaughter.*
couldn't have an affair with you, even if I'd wanted to
You and me? Having an affair? Here? Right under hi
nose? Besides, I wanted more than an affair, fa
more——'

'James, you were already having an affair.' It had to
be said. She couldn't even be sure that that affair had
finished. Oh, she understood, now, why he had held
back. She understood his point of view, his distaste a
the idea of having an affair with her because she was Si
Henry's granddaughter—and a woman who spoke only
in terms of wanting him physically but not in terms o
love.

'What on earth are you talking about?' He sat back
bemused.

'Diane Massey,' she said quietly.

'You don't—*What?*' James spoke the first words with
incredulity, the last word on a bark of laughter, and
now he was laughing his head off. 'I've never had an
affair with Diane! Not recently, not ever. I don't know
what put that idea into your head!'

'How can you say that?' Her voice went up and down
as if she were defending herself. 'I saw you together
right here, at Gramps' party, all lovey-dovey!'

'Oh, Debbie. Deborah.' He was only just beginning
to take her seriously. 'You saw—I don't know what
What you expected to see, perhaps. You invented the
rest, I assure you. Why, I'd *told* you she was just an old
friend. Is an old friend.'

'You—you're still seeing her?'

'From time to time, our paths will probably cross.'
And then he sobered, seeing the concern in her eyes.
'Darling, didn't she tell you what was in that box she
left for me? In any case, I should have thought its

contents were obvious.' When she looked at him
blankly, he smiled again because he couldn't help
himself. 'A piece of wedding cake. Her wedding cake.'

'Wedding cake? *Her*——'

'She got married last Saturday—to her ex-husband!
I've known him for years, too. I don't blame you for
looking at me like that. It's true!' He sighed, disturbed
by the incredulity on Deborah's face. 'Darling, it isn't
for me to talk about other people and their private lives
but, if it'll help to convince you, I'll just say that Diane
went through a very bad time when she got divorced.
She didn't want the divorce; she went through with it
only because that's what her pride dictated, her pride
but not her heart. I knew she was still in love with her
husband, and when I talked to him I learned that he felt
the same way. I acted as—as a go-between to a large
extent. But at first, all Diane needed was someone to
talk to, someone who would listen. We spent hours and
hours talking. Her husband——'

'No, James.' She stopped him, reaching for him as
she planted herself on his knee. 'Don't say any more.
She talked to you in confidence, and it has nothing to
do with me. I—I was wrong to doubt what you'd told
me and I . . . Oh, darling!'

She cuddled close to him, telling him how very
stupid she had been in so many ways. James just
laughed at that. His hand was on her leg, beneath her
skirt, making lazy circles on her thigh. 'What was
that?' he teased, 'Did you just say that you don't
know what I see in you? Well, come here. Closer,
Debbie, closer.'

He started whispering in her ear, and that's how
Bessie found them when she came to tell them dinner
was ready. Her thin grey eyebrows went up, her mouth
opened in a silent 'O' and she backed out of the room
very tactfully.

James and Deborah stifled their laughter until she

was safely out of earshot. 'Do you think she'll approve?' He put the question roguishly.

Deborah was still learning. She had been a slow starter in life and she still had plenty of catching up to do before she would attain the wisdom of James and her grandfather. But there was one thing she did know.

'Without a doubt.' Her tawny eyes were smiling at him. 'And I shouldn't be surprised to learn that Gramps once warned her this day would come. Would you, James?'

He answered her by kissing her on the nose, but she didn't mind. She didn't mind being Little Debbie from time to time, since that was only one of the things she would be to him—his wife, the mother of his children, his pupil, his confidante, his mistress . . . the woman he loved.

'What will we do at Christmas?' she asked, suddenly remembering her parents.

'Get married, of course,' he said, as if she'd asked an unnecessary question.

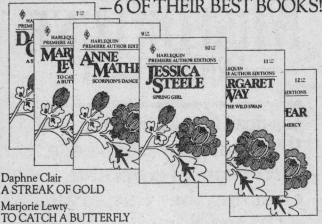

Harlequin reaches into the hearts and minds of women across America to bring you

Harlequin American Romance™

YOURS FREE!

Enter a uniquely exciting
new world with

Harlequin American Romance™

Harlequin American Romances are the first romances to explore today's love relationships. These compelling novels reach into the hearts and minds of women across America... probing the most intimate moments of romance, love and desire.

You'll follow romantic heroines and irresistible men as they boldly face confusing choices. Career first, love later? Love without marriage? Long-distance relationships? All the experiences that make love real are captured in the tender, loving pages of **Harlequin American Romances**.

What makes American women so different when it comes to love? Find out with **Harlequin American Romance!**

Send for your introductory FREE book now!

Get this book FREE!

Mail to:

Harlequin Reader Service

In the U.S.
2504 West Southern Ave.
Tempe, AZ 85282

In Canada
P.O. Box 2800, Postal Station A
5170 Yonge St., Willowdale, Ont. M2N 5T5

YES! I want to be one of the first to discover **Harlequin American Romance.** Send me FREE and without obligation *Twice in a Lifetime.* If you do not hear from me after I have examined my FREE book, please send me the 4 new **Harlequin American Romances** each month as soon as they come off the presses. I understand that I will be billed only $2.25 for each book (total $9.00). There are no shipping or handling charges. There is no minimum number of books that I have to purchase. In fact, I may cancel this arrangement at any time. *Twice in a Lifetime* is mine to keep as a FREE gift, even if I do not buy any additional books. **154 BPA NAZJ**

Name	(please print)	
Address		Apt. no.
City	State/Prov.	Zip/Postal Code

Signature (If under 18, parent or guardian must sign.)

AMR-SUB-3